Falling

Jack Dylan

Copyright © 2021 Jack Dylan.

All rights reserved. The characters and events portrayed in this book are fictitious. Any similarity to real persons, living or dead, is coincidental and not intended by the author. No part of this book may be reproduced, or stored in a retrieval system, or transmitted in any form or by any means, electronic, mechanical, photocopying, recording, or otherwise, without express written permission of the publisher.

ISBN- 9798506931829

CONTENTS

The Late Train 1
Good Morning Father...........................6
The Enby Experiment 14
The Fixer 24
Suspended 28
The Handshake 35
Empty Words 41
Breakthrough....................................46
The Tribe...61
Life: disrupted 69
The Accident 76
Julia 87
The Old Pub 94

The Late Train

The 10:58 was late, again. He fretted impotently on the platform amazed by the relaxed acceptance on the faces and in the postures of the other passengers. It always frustrated him how passively accepting of life's annoyances other people could be. His wife was a prime example. She could quietly accept that something had gone wrong with the car; the flight had been delayed; anything really, without feeling the need to blame someone or something, or the need to rage against it.

"There's nothing you can do about it so why get annoyed?" It was probably the most familiar refrain in their lives.

He looked at his watch, again. He checked it against the platform clock. A flicker of annoyance passed across his face when he saw there was a 30 second difference. He would check his watch that evening against the BBC time signal, but he was sure it was correct.

Two young males wearing hoodies came swearing down the platform. They interspersed every phrase with a thoughtless profanity. He wondered if they would be able to communicate without the use of the word. But surely they must have various events in their lives when it was important to speak properly? What about job interviews? "Well, quite," he thought.

Waves of disapproval emanated from him. The pursed lips, the frowning forehead, the piercing glare over the top of his reading glasses, all beamed out the message. It was his misfortune that the hooded youths picked up the message and did not like it at all.

They sat on the slatted wooden bench along the platform and lit part-smoked cigarettes. Most of the other travellers turned away from the defiance of the many 'no smoking' signs. One or two walked a little further away. But he was determined not to let it go by. Tucking his reading glasses carefully into their case, and folding his paper, he took a pace towards the bench. The larger youth returned a challenging look and with a toss of the head blew a cloud of smoke towards the wooden platform roof. The taunting test for him was mercifully interrupted by the announcement of the on-time arrival of his train. He was so outraged by the obviously inaccurate announcement that he decided to forget the delinquents for now. Pausing only to point at the No Smoking sign he threw a muttered 'Can't you read?' before turning away to board the train at his usual door.

He sat in his usual seat, gratified that this

routine was undisturbed. The two or three other regulars were there, but none acknowledged the others - it wasn't necessary. His paper was waiting, and he immersed himself in the cryptic crossword, his heavily engineered Rotring propelling pencil quickly and neatly entered the first few easy answers. The compiler was one of the more subtle and convoluted of the five or six the paper used, and his concentration was fully occupied by the clever twists and word-play.

The two hooded youths had noted where he sat, and were content to remain in the next carriage. They had to meet a man they referred to simply as 'Him' at lunchtime to collect the balance of the payment for a little job they had completed the previous night. The morning was theirs to enjoy as they liked, a pint or two most likely, and the powerful message of disapproval from the neatly suited man had triggered the smouldering and easily kindled rage that lurked below the casual surface.

He was unaware of the two following him from the station down the Strand, into Fleet Street, and then into the narrow steep alleys that were the short route to St Martins le Grand and his office. As he walked up past the empty coffee shops and the anonymous closed doors he was puzzling still over 12 across. There was a Greek mythical reference he was sure, but didn't want to look it up yet. He'd let his subconscious work on it for a while.

His right leg bent unnaturally at the knee. A scaffolding pole at full force on the outside of the joint burst the knee apart. He fell in a blinding haze of pain, and was only partly conscious of the nose-breaking crack of his attacker's knee as he fell. It was only a few minutes before another late commuter found him there and summoned the ambulance, but those few minutes were the most disturbing of his life. His leg lay at a sickening angle, every involuntary muscle movement sent bursts of pain more elemental than anything he had experienced. His broken and bloody nose was impeding his breathing, and he wondered if he was going to die.

Two months later he was still on crutches. They had been able to reconstruct the knee, but warned him not to expect 'full mobility' ever again. The bastards. Why him? He hobbled along the platform for the 10:58, no longer so incensed by the slight inevitable lateness. Relief at being able to resume some sort of normality had given him a more philosophical perspective on life and on priorities.

Two youths with grey hooded tops walked down the platform, smoking ostentatiously. Their eyes seemed to survey him with a look of some sort of smug amusement. He locked eyes with the bigger of the two and hoped he looked defiantly and properly challenging of their rule breaking.

"A'right Guv?" took him aback. The larger youth nudged his companion on the upper arm, and with raucous laughter they swaggered past him along the platform.

It was them. He suddenly knew it. They had been there smoking on the morning of his 'mugging' as the police called it. 'Crippling' would have been more accurate. What could he do? "They laughed, your Honour," did not sound like very definitive evidence against them. But the backward look he received from the two as he stared after them confirmed that they knew, and he knew, that there was nothing on this earth he could do about it.

Good Morning Father

"Good morning Father."

"Good morning Miss O'Connor. Good to see you out."

"I'd be here more often if the old legs would let me."

"Ah sure I know that. Just you let me know when you're having a bad time and I'll come to you."

"Thank you Father."

"Good morning Father."

"Good morning Mrs Moran, how's that new grandson doing?"

"The best, Father."

"Good morning Father."

"Good morning to you. (I wish I could remember that poor woman's name.)"

The scanty congregation from eight o'clock Mass filed out respectfully past the middle-aged Parish

Priest. He looked young for his forty-nine years, but the lines from smiles and sympathetic worries were etching their presence ever more deeply and permanently. Taking time to greet each member of the congregation – mostly elderly and mostly women - he took care to ask after the special cases he knew about that he could mention in public. Smiling warmly, he waited patiently for old Mr Molloy, who hobbled out last, his sticks clicking on the terrazzo floor. (Why didn't he get new rubber ferrules for those sticks?)

Father Maguire took pleasure in knowing his flock. He was sincerely interested in them, and believed that his work was beneficial in a social and practical way as well as in its primary spiritual function. He could see the benefit of the daily ritual in mundane ways – the structure it gave to the day; the sense of purpose to the early rising; the sense of achievement in attending; and the comfort from friendships as they nattered towards home.

He returned to the sacristy and thanked the two altar-boys who had already disrobed and were anxious to get away to school. The sacristan was waiting for him and helped hang the stole and robes on their wooden hangers.

"Not a bad crowd Father – for a Tuesday."

"No indeed Michael, not bad at all. I didn't see Mrs Murray there. Have you heard anything about her at all?"

"Not a word Father, but I'll check with the wife and let you know tomorrow."

"If there is a problem give me a ring later. If I need to go to see her this would be a good day to do it."

"I will surely. I'll see herself when I get home and I'll let you know."

"Thanks Michael. I'm not saying Mass again until tomorrow morning, so I'll see you then."

He walked contentedly the short distance home where his housekeeper would have breakfast waiting for him. He had persuaded her to give him fruit and yoghurt on weekdays. He wasn't a vain man, but the weight he saw in the mirror had started to worry him, and the slack skin when he shaved was a daily reminder of the passing years.

"You're getting old, John Maguire, and you'd better learn to live with it," he laughed silently, amused by the conflicting feelings that required him to fight for his healthy diet despite the well-ingrained antipathy to vanity.

He opened the varnished door with its old-fashioned stained glass panel. His jacket went routinely on its hanger, and he made his way down the dim hallway to the dining room. He thought again how thin the carpet runner felt on the old floorboards, but knew he had to live with it. The life was not supposed to be a luxurious one and there was little money for the likes of new carpets.

Rubbing his hands in mock anticipation he announced,

"Well Mrs Bradley, I'm looking forward to that fried soda. Did you get the black pudding?"

"The Bishop's secretary rang while you were out. He wants you at his office at ten."

"Is that all? Do I need to ring back?"

"I asked that and she said 'no'. The tea's ready and the fruit's in the bowl. I'll be off now and I'll do those dishes when I get back before lunch. Just leave them on the table."

She was off. He was curious and a little disquieted by the summons, but hoped it was a positive sign.

"I wonder is it the move to Dublin at last? Or is he going to offer me one of these new sabbaticals?"

He left the breakfast dishes as instructed and drove the little Toyota across town towards the Bishop's Palace. 'Palace' was a laughable misnomer. It was a dull, grey-rendered barracks of a house, surrounded by suffocating rhododendrons and exuding a sense of forbidding damp austerity. He was early and stopped for five minutes a short distance from the house to gather his thoughts.

"It's probably nothing significant. I shouldn't get my hopes up about the move. Probably just one of those routine 'clerical pastoral conversations' that are all the go now."

He drove in and parked on the dull grey gravel. He recognised the Bishop's car but not the other – a more expensive type than the Church usually thought appropriate. He rang the bell and was answered almost immediately by the Bishop's secretary.

"Could you wait here in the study Father," she didn't meet his eyes.

He waited ten minutes before the Bishop came in, with a grey-haired, grey-suited professional looking man in his wake.

"Thank you for coming Father Maguire. This is Mr Hanratty, the diocesan solicitor."

They awkwardly didn't shake hands. Hanratty nodded perfunctorily and affected not to notice the slight move that Father Maguire made to offer a hand.

The Bishop indicated a chair where he should sit, and took his own place in the black leather chair behind his desk. The solicitor sat at the end of the desk and opened his briefcase. The Bishop looked at his desk, checked his watch, opened his leather-bound notebook, cleared his throat several times, then began.

"Father Maguire. Mr Hanratty is here to record this meeting and will be taking notes as well as making an audio recording. I trust you have no objection." It wasn't a question.

Father Maguire's face reddened, and his knuckles whitened as he fought the sudden dizziness that threatened to overwhelm him. He cleared his throat but didn't speak.

"Father Maguire, allegations have been made against you by two individuals, and we have to take these allegations seriously."

"What have they said?" His voice was a hoarse whisper.

"They allege that during your time in Cloughfields, in the years 1990 to 1993, you abused your position of trust and had improper sexual contact with both complainants against their will, when they were aged thirteen and fourteen years respectively."

"Who are they?" He whispered.

"Mr Hanratty has recorded their allegations with me, and those signed statements have this morning been passed to the Police Service of Northern Ireland, who will now make arrangements to interview you and the complainants. They will investigate the issue and will search for any other complainants who have not yet come forward."

"This is not true." He struggled to clear his throat but the voice still emerged as a strangled whisper. "You know me. You know I am not like that."

"You will be aware that the Church's protocol is now very clear. You will be, in fact of this moment you are, suspended from Parish duties. You will reside at a house allocated by the Church and make yourself available to the Police when they require it. You will not communicate with anyone outside the house – which is incidentally not far from Antrim – and you must undertake to make no statements to the Press or to any other third party. Do you understand?"

He nodded.

"Can you please say you understand."

"No, I don't understand. I don't understand how you can take the word of two boys – if they are boys - who may have had some grudge against me, and throw away my life, my vocation. You can't do this. It is not right."

"You know that in the past we might have been able to reassign you elsewhere, or avoid public procedures, but it is very clear now that when allegations of this kind are made, the guilty, or rather the accused, must be suspended immediately and the police must be involved. We have no choice in the matter."

"Who are these boys, or men?"

The Bishop looked at Mr Hanratty who shook his head imperceptibly.

"If the police decide to act on the evidence you may or may not know who they are. They have a right to anonymity. Mr Hanratty will be acting on your behalf and will ensure that due process is followed."

"Mr Hanratty! With all due respect he is acting against me here. And he is also supposed to act on my behalf?"

"You must accept the way the Church sees fit to handle this. You took a vow to subject yourself to the discipline of the Church. That vow still binds you."

The Bishop had not prefaced his recent statements with 'Father'.

"You will also know that you are not permitted to perform Holy Rites during this time. You must not say the Mass nor take Confession, nor administer any other Sacrament. Do you understand?"

"No I don't understand. The Church has known me body and soul my whole life. You know I'm not guilty of this. How can you destroy everything like this?"

"Do you understand that you will reside in Antrim and that you are suspended from administering the Sacraments?"

"Yes."

"Mr Hanratty will accompany you to Antrim. We will arrange for your personal belongings to be brought there. That is all for the moment."

Hanratty clicked off the recorder, capped his pen, and snapped closed the briefcase. He stood and wordlessly indicated that Father Maguire should leave the room ahead of him. Their eyes met briefly. The cold, disapproving eyes hooded in folds of well-fed flesh looked quickly away. The other pair - bloodshot, tearful, - sought contact with the solicitor's eyes, and then with the Bishop.

The Bishop, lips pursed, concentrated on his

desk, closed his notebook and pushed it to one side.

The Enby Experiment

More aeons ago than I care to think of, our ancestors were fixated on the question of how we had evolved to our then state of sophistication and intelligence. Yes, we had plenty of fossil evidence and theories about 'spontaneous mutations' and 'persistence of advantage', but they didn't seem to get to the heart of what made us the sentient and creative beings that we are. It was for this reason that a number of experimental sites were created. They were designed to be self-contained eco-systems, where the conditions for carbon-based life were present and so far as possible were isolated from outside influence or interference.

For this latter reason they were located in an inconveniently distant cluster of planets, which made consistent observation difficult at the time. Nowadays of course we have the technology to overcome that disadvantage.

One site – a water dominated planet in a small system with a relatively stable solar orbit – proved to be the most conducive to prolific development of living creatures. The others had mixed fortunes. One in the same small solar system proved too hot and dry due to an imbalance in the atmospheric conditions. Others successfully hosted life but were vulnerable to external and internal events – solar flares; meteorite collisions; internal instability; atmospheric depletion – the list was a depressing reminder of the vulnerability of life in the fundamentally inhospitable universe.

In any case, the successful site became something of a cause celebre within the scientific and intellectual community. Debates raged about the extent of observation that should be permitted, and whether observation per se had an impact on the experimental site.

The result was that for many millions of their rotations, the peace of Wet-1 was relatively undisturbed. However in the last two-thousand rotations there has been an acceptance that, despite the downside of observing, there was otherwise no point in having established the experiment. Unless we observed and experimented there was no prospect of gaining insight into our own evolution.

What has become clear is that among the many millions of life forms that evolved there (and the number of surviving variants has in itself forced a rethink about 'persistence of advantage' theory) a counter-intuitive outcome has been that a land-based organism has become the dominant force in the eco-system. On a planet that is largely liquid-covered this is a surprising outcome. What has also been surprising is that the organism in question had achieved dominance despite being neither the biggest; the quickest; the strongest; nor even having the biggest brain. It has achieved this through learning to create implements and even complex systems of implements that overcome its limitations in size strength and speed. At a relatively early stage in the evolution of what became known as the 'Naked Biped' (NB or 'Enby'), they learned to create weapons that allowed them to kill creatures much bigger and stronger than themselves.

Early studies showed that Enbies were capable of communal cooperation but also of disastrous antagonisms and apparently mindless conflicts. This led to the development of the theory that Enbies do not have 'minds' as we know them, but simply react in either an intuitive or behaviourally learned pattern.

The issue of 'consciousness of the Enby' has been controversial. Some experts have taken the view that it is possible to have an intelligence that allows learning about what works and what doesn't (a kind of 'Persistence of Advantage' at a neural level) without the state that we think of as consciousness. They argue that if you combine enough organisms with this type of neural learning ability, what emerges is something that can be mistaken for conscious intelligent thought as we understand it.

One of the most intrusive and daring experimental interventions was called 'The Soul of the White Ant'. The theory was that if an analogy of Enby group culture were created and documented, genuinely conscious sentient Enbies would recognise the analogous descriptions and observations and be able to apply them to their own behaviour.

A sophisticated demonstration was established whereby the experimenters infiltrated an intelligent element into a host Enby and had him study in detail the behaviour of colonies of white ants or termites as they called them.

The experiment was a huge success. The study of the white ants was in itself interesting – demonstrating a communal level of co-operation and task achievement that taken as a whole could be described as intelligent behaviour, while not ascribing anything resembling intelligence to any one individual ant. The real success of the experiment lay in the reaction of other Enbies. Despite the findings being written up and carefully circulated – and yes, reading was one of the neural learning evolutions that had occurred – there was an almost total failure of Enbies to 'read across' or see the relevance of the study to themselves. This has been accepted for some time now as extremely strong evidence that whatever the complex systems that neural learning allows Enbies to create, fundamentally they lack what we would regard as a conscious intelligence, or as the popular tablets would have it – a mind.

It was decided at this time that further infiltrations of intelligence were justifiable for experimental reasons.

Note on Infiltration of intelligence:

The infiltration of an intelligent mind into an Enby was controversial. In the end every landmass and every country was provided with at least one 'animateur' who could propagate ideas of positive communal development. In some cases they were very successful in developing a following of 'believers', but their ideas and the progress resulting from them required a constant refreshment of newly infiltrated animateurs.

The same process was adopted in order to stimulate progress in science. Some of these experimentally introduced minds met with antagonism and even death. Others were more fortunate and were able to disseminate information and constructive ideas.

While these interventions disrupted the simplicity of the experiment, they were justified on the basis that there seemed little prospect of observable progress otherwise.

It is against this background that it was decided to document the behaviour and activities of Enbies against a number of key factors in order to support or disprove the 'Mindless Enby' hypothesis.

The factors were:

1. Evidence of logical systems of organisation and decision- making.
2. Actions leading to the greatest welfare of the greatest number.
3. Behaviour consistent with the preservation of the species.
4. Behaviour consistent with maintenance of the ecosystem supporting their life.

1: Logical systems of organisation and decision making:

Wet-1 had developed as a planet in such a way

that movements of its crust had established distinct units separated by water – some large, some small. This created the happy opportunity for a variety of observations and experiments with large and small populations of Enbies.

Our observations of the development of populations of Enbies followed similar patterns on both large and small landmasses.

Family groups accreted into tribal groupings. These tribes moved inexorably into a state of animosity with neighbouring tribes – each preferring to steal from the other; fight for disputed resources; and develop negative stories about the others. Cooperation or sharing was extremely rare until a larger tribe threatened both smaller units, in which case grudging cooperation against a shared enemy was possible.

This process continued over thousands of rotations until each landmass was a patchwork of countries, capable of cooperating only when jointly threatened.

To the frustration of the experimental observers, when they infiltrated an intelligent mind into an Enby who would promulgate ideas of progressive cooperation, the outcome was always the same. The subsequent potential partnerships between countries or even between tribes within countries were quickly frustrated by a majority inclination towards old antipathies.

The unfortunate conclusion after many painstaking observations was that Enbies are not capable of wholehearted genuine cooperation or of creating logical arrangements for government. No matter how small the unit there would inevitably be found divisions. And within each divided group there would be further division.

2: Activities leading to the greater welfare of greater numbers.

Our experimental observers infiltrated 'minds' who propagated the idea – phrased in various ways – that a good basis for deciding what course of action to follow would be to choose the option that had the most beneficial outcome for the greatest number of people.

Sadly, although the idea was welcomed, written in various forms into manifestos and constitutions, it was not acted out in practice. The observers were disappointed to find that a country could, with apparent sincerity, adopt the principle, but simultaneously organise the wealth and practicalities of the country to very blatantly favour a few and to disadvantage greater numbers.

3: Activities consistent with the preservation of the species.

This was perhaps the issue that led to the second-most decisive conclusion of the observers. Far from acting in ways that would preserve life, Enbies devoted great energy and sums of money to developing weapons designed to destroy life. As their technology became more sophisticated, (and here we must take some of the blame for infiltrating ideas and knowledge in the optimistic view that it would be used for logical and beneficial purposes) the weaponry they developed became more efficient at eliminating life. This reached the stage where antagonistic countries developed sufficient weaponry to wipe out not only their enemy but themselves also.

Their leaders seemed quite content to sentence vast numbers of their fellow Enbies to horrible deaths in the pursuit of whatever goal they had chosen, and sadly vast armies of Enbies willingly sacrificed themselves.

4: Behaviour consistent with maintaining the ecosystem that sustains life.

This was the issue that above all others convinced the observers that intelligent minds are not present in Enby society.

It must again be acknowledged that our experimental designers were excessively optimistic and took risks that in retrospect might have been better avoided.

The planet was provided with a primary energy source in the form of the solar body around which it orbits. The experimenters took the risk of allowing the development of alternative sources of energy. In their defence, they came from a point of view where the test of a child's intelligence might be that of offering a piece of bread or a stone to eat. Only the very deficient child would persist in trying to eat the stone.

Enbies discovered the energy possibilities of wood, coal, oil, gas, and the more scientifically sophisticated nuclear fuel. Each of these 'diversionary fuels' had manifest disadvantages either in terms of damaging Enby health, or in creating a negative impact on the atmospheric environment we ensured Enbies knew was essential for life.

As well as solar energy, the design of Wet-1 included swirling movements of fluid – air and water – that were intrinsic to the movement of the planet itself, and were augmented by a smaller orbiting body.

The experimental observers went to extreme lengths in infiltrating intelligent minds to divert Enby society from its self-destructive path. However it was only reluctantly, belatedly, and half-heartedly that they began to utilise solar and moving liquid resources. In a similar fashion to the other issues described above, their neural learning capabilities allowed them to develop sophisticated systems of extracting energy from all the diversionary sources, but did not allow them to think about the consequences. Our 'animateurs' appeared to have success in convincing some leaders of countries that they needed to take action if they were to preserve the environment necessary for life. Unfortunately the leaders appeared to react as if repeating the words and making some token gestures was sufficient, and real change was unnecessary or not possible.

Conclusion

It is with great reluctance that the Council has agreed that there appears to be no evidence of the development of intelligent minds on Wet-1. Therefore we have to conclude that the experiment has been a failure – unlikely to throw any light on the evolutionary processes that have brought our society and our individual and collective minds to their present state.

It must be reported that a minority view argues that the consistency of failure indicates the existence of intelligent minds. The argument is in essence that across all the observed factors, if there were no impact from intelligence, there should be a random distribution of positive and negative results. The complete consistency of negative results is an indication, in their view, of the existence and operation of intelligence. They concede that the intelligence is deployed in a self-destructive and illogical fashion, but maintain that it is there.

The Council has taken both the majority report and the minority view into account in coming to the decision to end the Wet-1 experiment and observations. There will be no further observation, and no further artificial infiltration of intelligence.

If the majority view is correct, the unintelligent management of the planet will lead to the elimination of Enby life.

If the minority view is in fact correct, the 'intelligent' management of the planet is so counter-productive and self-destructive that Enby life will be eliminated in any case.

Therefore the Wet-1 experiment is at an end, and unfortunately, fascinating though some of us find them, Enbies are to be left to self-destruct without further interference.

The Fixer

He fell backwards out of the window with a despairing curse. It was a sort of muttered, "ah fuck it," or perhaps, "you fucker," that sounded more like resigned annoyance than a death cry. It was of course in Russian, so the guttural sounds were even more expressive. He must have known that it was the end. The window was high up in the hotel, and below there was only the hard concrete paving of East 52nd Street. He would have instantly known it was a one-way ticket.

What was perhaps more surprising was that he didn't sound surprised. He sounded like someone who had espoused the inevitability of a violent death. Could it be that he was so familiar with the concept that it no longer held the terror that it would for any normal mortal?

The experiences of the man were the opposite of his immediate state. On how many occasions had he been the one left secure in the room while the victim screamed their last descent? He was a violent man. Always had been. He had been violent in a sneaky, calculating way. His stature meant that he picked his moments with care. He weighed around a half of many of his victims. He had the thin, wiry, desiccated looking body of the lifelong smoker, who ate out of necessity rather than pleasure. So he never picked a fair fight. He had to strike once, and decisively. His preferred method was the fall. It meant no bullet that could be traced to a weapon; no wound that could be matched to a knife.

When he was demobilised from the Russian army following the chaotic retreat from Afghanistan, he took with him a reputation for careful, definitive violence. There had been none of the barracks brawling; none of the drunken fist fights or occasional knife fights that were the inevitable consequence of cooping up crowds of disgruntled fighting men in the same camp. His reputation was more sinister and more unequivocal. Men talked in muted conversations about the corporal suspected of cheating him at cards. There was no fight, no threat, in fact no words at all. But next day the corporal did not return from his patrol, and everyone knew that the thin soldier, - the fixer - whose hard gaze few could meet, had been the executioner.

His position was protected by his superiors because he was the fixer. He could procure most things they needed that were unavailable from the official stores. Fine wines, proper sausage, real French brandy - all secured his position with his superior officers. They did not want to know his methods, and the balance of guilt meant that they deflected any hint of investigation into the deaths that sometimes coincided with his activities. No one questioned him. No one was willing to take the risk of accusing him. The hard, cold eyes in the smoker's lined face conveyed a message of absolute clarity. If anyone were to take him on it would be at their own risk - because if they didn't get a conclusive result, they would never again be able to relax.

His only apparent friend was physically, and in every other way, his opposite. Yuri was nicknamed 'the Bear'. His bulk was intimidating enough, but the muscular power in his body would have suited a circus strongman. He could pick up a normal man with one hand. The hand was almost the size of a man's head, and the knuckles were scarred hard and apparently felt no pain. Yuri was devoted to the little wiry smoker for reasons that no one could fathom. He took orders from no one else. He cast a look in the smoker's direction when someone asked him to help with a camp duty. The imperceptible nod was the necessary signal.

Yuri left the army with the fixer, and the symbiotic relationship flourished in the 'might is right' atmosphere of the disintegrating Soviet Union. No one but Yuri knew what brutal disposals the fixer was responsible for, as they worked for many masters. Money was plentiful, and they lived as they liked, with access to the pleasures and distractions of the world of the wealthy.

Yuri built up a considerable bank balance. It was, he realised, enough to see him comfortably off for the rest of his life. He was a simple man:

straightforward in his thinking and in his way thoughtful. He enjoyed the relationship with the fixer, but in his straightforward analysis, the fixer was both his meal-ticket and his nemesis. No one but the fixer could or would dare to stand as witness against him, no one else had the detailed knowledge of the beatings, the torture, the assassinations that they had expertly completed.

Yuri thought a lot about this. The fixer was the one with the connections. He knew the corrupt officials, the fantastically wealthy businessmen, and the politicians who had used their services. If anyone was able to 'cut a deal' and achieve some sort of amnesty for himself it could only be him. Yuri did not have the access.

Yuri imagined that like him, one day the fixer would decide enough was enough. Old age, too much vodka, too many cigarettes, too weary a body, would prompt the fixer to decide to end his career. Yuri could not know when that might happen. He knew for sure that he wouldn't see it coming, for the fixer would not leave loose ends. Yuri's straightforward thinking came to the only rational decision that was possible.

Suspended

He drifted helplessly in a state somewhere between sleep and hazy thought. Dreams were almost indistinguishable from thoughts, especially since he had started to dream that he was awake and unable to sleep. It had taken him weeks to realise what was happening, as it was only the presence of obviously erroneous detail in the 'lying awake' dream, like looking at the watch he no longer wore, that convinced him it had truly been a dream.

A carbon-fibre-reinforced umbilical cord was the only thing connecting him to the surface. It fed nutrients and re-oxygenated blood directly into his body. The other tubes dealt efficiently with the 'waste' as they had euphemistically called his excretions.

He felt confused. It seemed as if the thought process that had allowed him to identify the 'lying awake' dream as a dream, might itself have been a dream. The logic started to defeat him. Too many layers of possibility. Too many disturbing possibilities. If they were both dreams, was he still in any wakeful sense in touch with reality?

He had panicked when the implant in his brain flashed up the 'low power' warning. How long ago was that? Hours? Minutes? The implant was supposed to monitor his vital signs and to ensure that 'they' were keeping track of him. If the implant failed, they wouldn't know if he was alive or dead. If they had allowed the implant's power to become so low were they still there?

The sensory deprivation tank was designed to be a guaranteed way of inducing the worry-free relaxation that was part of the deal. He had imagined that it would be a fuzzily pleasant experience drifting off for who knew how long, until the conditions for 'revival' were met. In his case the conditions included an absolutely guaranteed cure for the disease that otherwise would have ended his life before now.

He had considered the cryonic option, but the idea of completely freezing his head and brain had made him uneasy. The supposed demonstration video had left him unimpressed, and the salesmen struck him as more suited to selling used cars than life-preserving technology.

The ultra-slow hibernation option had appealed because he could understand it better. Bears did it every year. It was easier to imagine a brain in deep resting state coming back to life than it was to imagine the ice crystals in a brain melting away to leave the organ functioning.

But the dreams and thoughts were not slowing

down as they should. How long was it now? It seemed an eternity, but there was no way of telling the date or the time. The salesman had sold this as a benefit; part of the process of achieving the state of totally relaxed hibernation that would slow every bodily process to less than a tenth of normal speed. It meant that his heart, his liver, all his other organs, even the wrinkles on his face, would age at less than one tenth of normal speed. Since without the disease he could have expected to have at least another thirty years of life, it meant that he could expect three hundred years of slow hibernation before it became irrelevant if they had found a cure.

He had worried about the support system breaking down. They had reassured him about the multiple redundancies built in to the automatic systems that kept the supply intact. What had the convincing salesman said? Something like, "We've calculated that even if no one looked at the system and all external power systems were down, the back-up systems would continue functioning for ten years at least."

He imagined the possibility that the world that he knew had ceased to exist. What if there were no one left in that glass and stainless steel control room? He knew that the disturbing thoughts were counteracting the supposed slow-down of his systems. He shouldn't be able to feel the fear and occasional panic that had started to invade his time. No day, no night, only time. And no way of measuring it. No reference points of any sort.

What had they told him about the emergency signal? Did he dream that there was one? In his previous life he would have noted it in his iPhone's contact book under 'E' for emergency.

Relax. Try a pleasant dream. They told him to avoid sexual fantasies - too stimulating - but the prohibition was almost the worst thing they could have done. Like telling a child, 'Here's a cupboard that you are not allowed to open. Open any of the others but not that one with the tempting coloured door and the big handle'. He thought, or did he dream that he thought, about his ex-wife? He could feel the agitation take a grip of his supposedly relaxed body.

He slept. He woke. Or did he. He was in a panic in the dream because he was awake and couldn't sleep. It seemed little different from being asleep and unable to waken. He had forgotten the panic code. He couldn't get out of here. Why was the implant low on power? Why had no one intervened?

He started to put theories together about what might have happened. The first theory was that it was a simple software glitch. The low power warning was just an error that the technician would have noted and corrected with a few deft taps on a keyboard. That was probably it. They had explained how he could see 'in his mind's eye' the message from the implant. A bit like recalling a face you know, or a view that you are familiar with. The clarity can vary, according to what your brain is doing - the more sleepy the state the clearer the picture - but the message would present itself in plain English. Perhaps he had dreamt the message. What was the last definite message he could recall?

Shit. How could he know what was an imagined message and what was a real one? If it used the brain's image creation ability, how do you distinguish implant from imagination?

He could feel his agitation whittling away the 300 theoretical years he had invested in. The more he thought about it the more agitated he became and the faster he lost time from the suspended animation total. They had explained to him how mental agitation automatically speeds up all the autonomic systems, pushing his ageing process back towards normal speed. "Don't worry," they had said, "if we see it happening we'll add a little something to the nutrients that will make things easier." No sign of that. Which confirmed his nagging fear that there was no one 'up there', he was no longer being monitored. He was probably going to rapidly end his days in this bizarre chamber, cut off from the world and beyond rescue.

He tried to move his arms or his legs - something to overcome the feeling of total helplessness. He visualised his brain sending the messages to the muscles. He willed the limbs to move. He almost shouted at his arm to move, to hit out, but he could neither shout out nor move. He was conscious of willing of the limb to move, but after that nothing. It seemed like a paralysis that he had no means to overcome. He wanted to cry, but couldn't.

They had joked with him that the chamber could withstand a nuclear attack, an earthquake, a tsunami, and a volcanic eruption - and he had politely laughed at the outlandish examples of catastrophes they all knew weren't going to happen. What was the name of the dictator in that far eastern state? He had threatened the West when he came to power. What if it hadn't been what the television commentator described as the 'domestically expected rhetoric'? What if he had meant it?

Right, he thought to himself, I'm going to stop imagining the worst and start to relax so I get back to the slow resting state that I've spent my life savings achieving. Get a grip. Stop allowing these foolish fantasies to disrupt the process.

'Implant power critical. About to shut down.' The words seemed unquestionably real in his mind's eye. They were gone now, but unless he was really losing it they had been there, quite clearly readable in that odd Tahoma font the machine used. But of course they would look like that if he dreamed them. Was it Descartes who wrote about how we distinguish dreams from reality? Something about the vividness of the experience? All very well in theory. Descartes hadn't thought about the context of a sensory deprivation tank and a chemically induced slow hibernation, where there was no external stimulation against which to compare the experience.

There must be no one left up there. He was now convinced. Perhaps it had been a nuclear attack. Perhaps a more straightforward disaster like a serious fire that had taken out the control room. Had there been a back-up plan for that scenario? Of course there would have been. Maybe it was the earthquake, the 'big one'. This being the west coast, the long awaited mega earthquake might have come at long last. If it was as bad as the doomsayers predicted, the rescue operations would have higher priorities than a highly secretive facility that sounded not unlike the crackpot cryogenic installations that had been ripping off the rich for decades.

He felt rather than heard a click. It couldn't

have been a click. Solid-state electronic implants have no moving parts. It felt like something switching off. He held his breath, and the fast beat of his heart wiped more years from the supposed hibernation. He waited, tense, listening. Nothing.

The Handshake

He was walking home carrying a bundle of bamboo canes. The garden vegetables were growing fast and the peas had already required all his existing canes.

Arthur was retired, but prided himself on looking years younger. The combination of work in the garden, plenty of walking and visits to the gym had kept him in good physical shape. Today's shopping trip was indicative of the way he lived. Rather than take the car, he had travelled by train and bus to the garden centre to buy the canes and the few extra packets of seed he needed.

As usual, he had picked up his morning paper on the way, and had passed the time contentedly reading the news, snorting at the latest government pronouncements, and starting the concise crossword. The walk from the bus stop to the garden centre was short, and he had organised himself to complete his shopping and be back at the opposite bus stop in time for the returning bus. Most people thought of him as the epitome of the organised man. His habits were regular; his house and garden were neat and tidy; and his dealings with the rest of the world were measured, careful and honest.

Today he wore his casual 'out of the house' clothes – a well-washed check woollen shirt, moss coloured corduroy trousers, and a slightly drooping sports jacket. The pockets causing the droop were home to a selection of 'just in case' items. He disliked being without the old penknife that he had used for many years. The timetables for bus and train were always present. A muesli bar ensured that he wouldn't go hungry even if delayed. An old mobile phone was there not because he had any intention of using it, but because his daughters insisted that he should carry it. He often omitted to check if it was turned on, to their great frustration.

As he walked back from the station towards home, he was aware of a group of teenagers behind him apparently following his path. It didn't worry him at first, as the town was a peaceful one, and most of the teenagers were not of a threatening type. They generally fitted his term of 'disaffected youth', which meant that their clothing was sloppy and their gait slouching. They seemed to spend their time comparing posts on expensive mobile phones or kicking around aimlessly with earphones in their ears. He felt a certain amount of pity for them, as they seemed to be without purpose or structure to their days.

His own life had always been structured and planned. The careful progression up the ranks in the civil service had followed a reassuringly predicable and satisfactory pattern. He needed to remind himself sometimes that it hadn't always been as straightforward as that. There had been disappointments and delays, but overall it had been an extremely predicable if not high-flying career. So his retirement had brought the index linked pension and a feeling of secure and potentially pleasurable times.

Arthur's wife Angela had died almost fifteen years earlier, when the girls had already left home for their respective careers and marriages. One now lived only an hour's drive north, but the other had moved to Cornwall and was an infrequent visitor. He had adjusted well to his single life. For ten years after Angela's death he was still working full time, and had plenty of company during the day. During the early years after the death, both daughters had been living within easy reach, and they ensured that weekends were busy for him. While he of course missed her, he hadn't been as devastated by Angela's death as most people seemed to expect. Nor had it left him feeling as alone and purposeless as some widowers obviously felt. His friends were not surprised at this, as they recognised how self-contained he had always been. They knew that he was very content to spend time quietly with a book and some music.

Arthur was not as conservative as many of his old colleagues had been. His approach to life was more liberal and accepting. His politics had always leaned towards the left and his voting had depended on his view of the current Labour leader. He often surprised his daughters when he expressed opinions sympathetic to single mothers, disadvantaged children, asylum seekers, and all the other categories of people unlikely to inhabit the golf club. He told them that his time volunteering in Citizens Advice had left him with an understanding of how easily people could fall out of the mainstream of polite and secure society.

So it was with a relatively unprejudiced eye that he observed the disaffected youths following his path. His natural assumptions tended towards straightforward innocent explanations rather than fearing the worst. When he read in the paper of some young people vandalising a statue, he was more likely to wonder what had driven them to feel that this was a good idea than to complain about 'modern youth'.

As he turned the corner from Station Road into the quiet street leading towards home, he heard a coarse young voice shout, "Hey gramps." He ignored it at first, largely because he didn't think of himself as 'gramps', and also because he didn't expect to be addressed. As he walked on towards the junction of the quiet side street with the wider suburban avenue, he became conscious of the footsteps of the group of youths close behind. He continued to walk at the same pace, not exactly worried, but starting to feel a little uncertain. He resisted the urge to turn round to face them.

Suddenly the bamboo canes were whisked from his grip. One of the hooded youths waved them around, laughing at Arthur's shocked face. The other four encircled him and said, "Sorry gramps, he's a bit of a tosser."

"That's OK," Arthur responded, "If you'll just give me the canes back I'll get home and get on with my tasks."

"How much did they cost gramps?"

"Not much. Just a couple of pounds."

"That's fair enough. Give us a couple of quid you can have 'em back."

Arthur's liberal and non-confrontational nature was having a tough time. The youths were sneering and unpleasant. They were less and less like the 'basically good lads, just a bit aimless' that was his usual default opinion. There was no one else around. The street was quiet, so there was no one to look to for help.

"Now look here," he heard himself start. Not the way the usual Arthur would mean to engage with a teenager. "I don't know what you're after but I'm afraid I'd like my belongings back and we can all go on our way."

"Tell you what gramps," the spokesman for the group responded. "You give us the cash and we'll leave you alone. Can't be fairer than that, eh?" The lad with the canes had by now broken one while flailing around in a pretend fight with a lamppost. The other three obviously looked to the spokesman as their leader, and were smirking at Arthur, who was clearly at the mercy of their man.

"Look here lads, what do you need the money for? I would like to get going and I don't want any fuss."

"You give me a fiver and that's us square. Beezer, bring those sticks over here."

"OK. This is outrageous, but fair enough. If that's what it takes to get home quickly here's a fiver." He started to reach into the inner jacket pocket for his wallet."

"OK gramps. Shake on it then." The youth

held out his right hand while the other youths grinned.

Arthur decided he might as well go through with the charade, and with his left hand still feeling for the wallet, held out his right hand. The youth in a quick move grabbed Arthur's hand and pulled him forcefully forward. At the same time he lunged forward with his forehead and butted Arthur hard on the nose. There was a crack and blood started spurting out. Arthur felt himself pushed roughly to the ground, and half a dozen hands seemed to be simultaneously searching his pockets. A moment later they were gone. The bamboo canes were scattered around him on the ground.

Arthur tried to reach his handkerchief to stem the blood, and at the same time tried to raise himself onto a knee as the first stage in getting up again. His face hurt abominably, his shirt and jacket were stained with blood, and he suddenly felt dizzy and weak.

He was poised one hand on the ground and one to his face when help arrived.

"Young tearaways," said a sympathetic voice. "Happens all the time here. Did they get your wallet?"

"Bastards," said Arthur. "Should be locked up.

Empty Words

"Thanks"
"Have a nice day sir, and hope to see you again soon."
"You will. Back in a couple of weeks."
"You take care sir."
He picked up his overnight case and slung the heavy laptop bag over his shoulder. The empty formula of hotel reception greetings grated more annoyingly than ever. He accepted rationally that the insincere words were part of the formulaic exchanges that eased the need for thought and genuine conversation. With two hundred guests to check out each day the receptionist couldn't be interested in what sort of day each of them had, never mind whether he would see them again or not. So the easy empty words he had been trained to use were the modern

politenesses that gave a veneer of human contact to the otherwise mechanical and electronic process of assigning a charge to the hundreds of company credit cards. But he despised the words and the automaton that uttered them. Even more so he despised the system and the company that manufactured the pretence of warm friendly contact. However he knew he might as well complain about television newsreaders signing off with an insincere hope that they would "see" him again tomorrow. At least there was no patent illogicality in the receptionist's words – just mindless emptiness and insincerity. He blamed the hotel chain culture.

He swung the white Vauxhall Insignia out of the hotel car park, grimly noting the number of identical cars that littered the area, all chosen by fleet managers because white was the colour that incurred no extra cost, and Insignias because Vauxhall were out-discounting Ford in fleet sales. It depressed him.

He used to be able to choose his laptop. Now they all had basic Lenovo 15 inch models. They were painfully heavy to lug around, but they were the company's standard pre-configured model – carefully set up in a way that prevented the addition of any of his own software. The company's sales material, order forms, visit schedules, expense forms, and 'employee information bulletins' were automatically updated and exchanged when he connected the machine to the internet. They had built in filters to the internet browser which precluded the old habits of late night soft porn browsing. He knew that the IT department would log the browsing that he did anyway, so it was a strong disincentive to indulge in anything that might be embarrassing.

He felt emasculated – no more than an identikit salesman, as easily replaced as a faulty Insignia or Lenovo. His sales figures were good, but that was simply a function of the area he covered and the effectiveness of the marketing department's stimulation of demand. He wondered why the company still employed people like him when the process could so easily be automated. It struck him that perhaps he was cheaper than developing and installing the necessary software in all the customer terminals. How long before that equation changed?

It proved to be surprisingly easy to acquire the credit card. The utility bills for his false address had been remarkably easy to create. It seemed as if the security systems had been designed before document creation and printing featured in every private house.

Business cards were easy. The hotel even had a machine in the foyer where you could design and print twenty for a fiver. It gave him a special frisson of pleasure to use their machine.

He felt more alive than he had done in months. A plan had started to emerge as he drove the numbing motorway miles – directed by the company sat-nav on the most cost-effective route. He found himself smiling when he added another sophistication or detail to the plan. It was as if his sales job had provided him with all the insight he needed to hotel systems and procedures. He also knew how important conference business was to the hotels. They could break even on room rental costs and make their profit from the bar takings generated by hundreds of socialising, or rather 'networking' business-people.

He chose a hotel from the chain his company used, but well outside his sales area. Living in the midlands and having a territory that was immutably defined – think of all the system and reporting changes that would ensue if the sales areas were amended – he chose the hotel chain's top location in Wales.

The 'conference' had a grandiose title – 'Marketing Solutions for the Networked Age'. The hotel agreed to reproduce his invented company logo on their menus and welcome packs. He knew that the champagne reception for 200 guests and a two-night conference would have the manager salivating and building the anticipated profit into his forecasts. The guest list would be handled by his company and provided to the hotel once finalised, with executive rooms requested for the top twenty delegates.

He said he represented an event management company – working on behalf of his actual company. He knew that the hotel would not bother to check with the actual company that he was acting on their behalf. A two-hundred person two-day event for a household name company was not particularly unusual, and was almost invariably organised by an external event management expert. The two thousand pound deposit went through easily on the illicit card, and the failure to pay would not be flagged up for another six to eight weeks.

The real company staff list provided all the names required. The directors and senior managers were allocated the executive rooms. The main conference room was booked along with five smaller rooms for breakout sessions.

His imagination soared. He invented speakers, keynote address titles, and discussion group subjects. He ensured that the hotel would have the latest data-projectors and electronic white-boards. The conference manager and he became co-conspirators, agreeing the dinner wines; the vegetarian options; the free bar limit; the timing of coffee breaks; the budget for Danish pastries rather than the usual biscuits; the brand of champagne for the reception; and even the provision of a local toastmaster for the formal dinner.

It seemed real to him. It was the most creative work he had completed in years. The hotel was completely dedicated to the conference. A number of regular customers had been apologetically re-assigned to a neighbouring hotel, and booking staff had for weeks been turning down bookings for the chosen dates.

On the evening of the delegate arrival and champagne reception he drove slowly past the hotel. The only car in sight had flashing blue lights and the North Wales Police logo.

The car park did not contain a single white Vauxhall Insignia.

Breakthrough

I lifted my gaze from the half-completed page of another futile attempt at a short story and saw a boat sailing slowly towards me round the headland. My pencil hovered over the paper while I concentrated on the arrival in the anchorage. It was a neat-looking converted fishing boat. The hull was painted white and the new topsides were glowing varnished pine. A short mast, a sail neatly flaked on the boom, and a furled foresail promised at least the possibility of sailing rather than motoring. The polished bright-work glinted in the warm Turkish morning sunlight, and spoke of daily polishing and care.

I could see someone on the aft deck, sitting under the shading canvas, but also – unnecessarily I thought – wearing a wide-brimmed straw hat. The hat was unmistakeably female. A crewman looked out of the open door of the varnished cabin then ducked back inside to the wheel.

It was unusual for these hired tourist boats, as I supposed it to be, to approach slowly. Usually they headed briskly for their chosen spot, dropped anchor with practised confidence, reversed briskly towards the shore, and sent a boy ashore in a noisy dinghy to rig a stern line. This one seemed in no hurry. I guessed they had been sailing and just furled the sails before coming into view, letting the momentum carry them into my sheltered bay. No engine noise disturbed the cicadas chirping in the scrubby trees ashore. Variegated with pine, olive and myrtle, the green hillside looked on undisturbed.

Another head appeared on the aft deck. This one wore a nautical peaked cap. An affectation, I immediately thought, of the type favoured by men of a certain age indulging a fantasy about being an 'old salt', while nothing could be further from the truth.

The boat continued to turn, clearly heading for my anchorage. As it progressed further into the bay the aft deck became more clearly visible, and I could see that the couple were at either side of a deck table, the woman sitting in a comfortable director's chair, the man standing, hands in jacket pockets – Prince Charles style. A jacket! In fact it looked like a blazer. At this distance I couldn't see if there was a crest on the breast pocket, but I would have bet a lot of money that there was.

A crewman appeared on the foredeck, and with a metallic clang let go the anchor. The chain rattled out as the boat continued its gliding progress into the bay. I admired the fuss-free confidence of the approach and the ease with which the two crew seemed to manage. It was in stark contrast to my own cautious testing out; checking depths; looking for alternatives, and finally carefully anchoring.

I heard a voice called out a word, possibly 'Tamam', and the rattle of the chain stopped. The bow was checked by the pull of the chain and the boat pivoted neatly through 180 degrees. The stern passed by giving me a clear view of the passengers. The man, probably forty metres away, appeared to nod perfunctorily in my direction. The woman continued reading.

A splash alerted me to the crewman diving from the stern of the boat, a line tied round his body. He swam the short distance to the shore, deftly tied the rope to the base of an olive tree, and swam back to the boat.

The capped man watched with an air of supervisory approval as the crewman hauled in the slack in the stern line. In a minute it was tight and the boat was secure. It was the most elegantly efficient operation I had seen for weeks.

I gave a mock salute, which I hoped they would interpret as admiration or approval, and was rewarded by a definite nod from the cap. The bay returned to stillness. The ripples from the arrival exhausted themselves on the rocky shore, and the crew continued to tidy the ropes on the deck of the pristine little craft. I found myself more in admiration of the whole outfit than was my norm. Daily or weekly charter boats from the nearby large harbours often had noisy and hard-working diesel engines that dominated the bay while they worked. I was impressed by the very different style of this boat. I was also intrigued by the incongruous blazer-wearing passenger, and equally by the nonchalant straw-hatted woman, who gave the impression of having walked straight out of a 1930s American movie. I decided that this was in fact the couple's private yacht rather than a tourist rental.

I returned to my writing, determined to stick to my resolution to write for at least two hours each morning. The discipline was a necessary substitute for inspiration.

I was alone on my yacht as it was my habit to have friends or family out for three or four weeks, then to dispatch everyone home so that I could have a few weeks of peace, ostensibly to write. Unspoken also was the quiet opportunity to relax, forget about normal duties and restrictions, and see what might turn up.

My previous books had failed to get past the first hurdle of exciting an agent, and I knew I was at a point where I might have to face realities and stop the pretence of being a 'writer'. I had enough money to get by in any case, and the writing was an indulgence that gave some purpose and focus to my work-free status. I referred to myself as having been 'invalided out' of my company, but my health was now as robust as anyone over fifty can hope for, and the yacht was my main extravagance.

I buried myself again in the pages of turgid rubbish I seemed to turn out, but the childhood-instilled discipline kept me at it for the regulation two hours.

"I say." The voice surprised me. It was the 'blazer and cap' individual sitting on the thwart of a little clinker-built rowing boat. He had forsaken the cap and blazer, and wore a crisp white shirt and those pinkish cotton trousers that seem to be the uniform of the South Coast English sailor.

He had approached soundlessly, which told me something of his skill with an oar.

"I say." This time he had my attention and continued, "Couldn't help noticing you seemed to be alone. Wondered if you fancied joining us shortly for a glass of something cold?"

He sounded like an American acting the part of an English gentleman. The accent fell somewhere between the popular 'mid-Atlantic' and a refined professorial US. It was well-modulated, crisp, polite, and immensely proper.

"That's very kind. I'd be delighted. What time do you suggest?"

"As soon as you like. Sun's over the yardarm as they say."

"I'll be there in fifteen minutes if that's OK."

"Perfect. See you then."

He backed one oar, pulled with the other, and spun the little dinghy round. He rowed silently and expertly back to what I now was sure was his private motor-yacht.

I busied myself stowing my writing things and had a quick wash before hunting out the cleanest t-shirt and shorts I could find. Living alone on board I didn't have to be too fussy, but kept a few clean things – just in case.

Fifteen minutes later I nudged gently alongside the motor-yacht, careful to keep the oars from knocking the unmarked hull. I was very conscious of the well-used look of my dinghy, not to mention myself.

"Jolly good. Pass me the painter and come

aboard. Now what will it be? G&T? Chankaya? Pimms perhaps?"

"G&T would be perfect."

"Darling, another G&T for …?" He looked quizzically at me to insert the missing name."

"Jack. Jack Drummond."

"Ah, of course. For Jack, dear," he called down the companionway.

"Vernon. Vernon Appleby"

Vernon's wife appeared with one of those non-slip trays holding three long clinking gins and a little dish of olives. She was dressed in a loose cream linen shirt and trousers. The tanned skin looked seductively smooth above the shirt buttons, and I could see an alluring glimpse of small tanned breasts as she delivered the gin. I immediately averted my eyes, reminding myself how unacceptable it was to ogle a man's wife.

"Thanks, that looks wonderful. I'm afraid I can't manage ice in my little fridge."

"Makes all the difference doesn't it. Jack, this is my sister Veronica; Veronica, Jack Drummond."

"Good to meet you."

"Our pleasure." She fixed me with a look that struck me as more than routine politeness. There was a wry challenge, a hint of amusement, and a clear element of appraisal in those dark, not quite demure eyes.

I forced myself to focus on Vernon.

"Lovely boat you have here. I take it she is your own?"

"Thank you. Yes, we had her built last year in the old boatyard in Fethiye. I wanted the old style but with up-to-date equipment. They made a good job of it, and she sails decently – as the original fishing boats this shape had to do of course."

"I must congratulate you on your crew's seamanship. That was the neatest approach I've seen all year."

"Ah, thanks. I find that once they know the standard you want these local chaps are quite up to it. As you may have noticed, I supervise but don't interfere. They know what I like."

"Very impressive."

"But what about you? Don't you find it tricky doing everything on your own?" She was looking at me and leaning forward slightly as if genuinely interested.

I kept my eyes on her face.

"I'm used to it. Really just a matter of taking time to prepare things in advance and thinking out how you're going to do it."

"Like many other things in life." I wasn't sure if this was a question or a comment on something specific, but decided it probably related to something the two had been discussing before, so I let it pass.

The drinks went well. We chatted about the area; our favourite bays; the rising cost in the tavernas; the unreliability of the weather forecasts – mostly the sort of things that sailors chat about when they meet. Throughout it all I was conscious that Veronica was attentive but had the air of waiting to turn the conversation in a different direction.

"So, I hear you are a writer, Jack."

"Well a struggling one. Not a very successful one."

"It can't be too bad if you can manage this." She indicated the bay, the yacht, the circumstances, with a little inclination of her head."

"If only," I confessed. "This is the result of past life rather than present efforts."

"Sounds idyllic anyway. And in case you are wondering, Ramazan told us all about you last night. You can't expect any privacy when the locals know all about you."

Ramazan was an old friend who ran a little taverna in the next bay. I made a practice of spending a few nights there, as he was friendly, and a good man to know if you needed help.

"Don't believe everything Ramazan says. He likes to think I'm more successful than I really am. I could do with him as my publicist back home."

"No false modesty please Jack, I know you are very successful."

I smiled and shook my head.

I returned later to my yacht, for the customary afternoon doze. The gin had given way to chilled white wine, (the Chankaya Vernon had offered) along with some local mezes and bread. I felt as if I was dining in unaccustomed style. All the while Vernon chatted amiably about yachting, about American politics, and about UK politics – about which he seemed well informed. Veronica played the part of a very able partner – a well-practised mixed doubles. She injected some humour; paid attention to me; asked questions; occasionally silenced her brother so that I could speak; and made me feel more interesting than I had any right to be. I rowed back in a warm glow.

Of course we had dinner on the Meltemi – a slightly strange name I thought, after the Aegean wind that sweeps all before it. They were moving on the next day for some pressing reason, but we exchanged contact numbers and emails amid promises of meeting the next time they were in London.

I finished my solitary spell ten days later, and flew back to London with more hope than expectation of meeting the delectable Veronica again. I couldn't get those eyes and that perfect skin out of my mind. There had been no physical contact with her at all. I realised we had not even shared a handshake, never mind a kiss on the cheek. Perhaps that had added to the allure – the untouched, untouchable perfection.

I searched for the perfume she had worn – pestered the girls in Selfridges to try to identify it. I knew it was utterly illogical, but it reflected the increasing fixation I had with the elusive Veronica.

In November I had an email from her. She was to be in London the following week – Christmas shopping – no mention of Vernon.

We met. That long denied touch was as electric as my foetid imagination had built it up to be. In effect I threw myself at Veronica, and she more that fulfilled my imaginings. I was in love, and for some bizarre reason this perfect, intelligent woman was interested in me. She loved my writing. She had friends in publishing in New York. Her oldest school-friend was married to a well-known agent. I began to see fate taking a hand in my struggling career. I arranged to email her a few short stories and the first chapters of the frequently rejected novel.

During the course of the week it emerged that

her brother was a very successful fund manager in New York – hence the ability to indulge his sailing fantasy. She didn't labour it, but I learned enough to be impressed by his success as well as by his previous modesty. She mentioned the name of his company and when I Googled it found an impressive web-site which indicated extremely impressive fund management. 'The sage of New York' I thought.

In my self-deprecating way I confessed to Veronica the dreadful investment performance of the money I had received on selling my equity in my old company. It had marked time and then dropped in value much to my annoyance. She sympathised but left it at that.

At the end of a gloriously frenetic week she returned to New York. We arranged that when her publishing friends had a chance to read my extracts I might, no I would, fly to New York to meet them. The prospect of a week or two in New York left me in a barely controlled frenzy of anticipation.

She phoned a week later, updated me on who she had given my writing to, and made encouraging comments about the prospects of meetings.

"Darling you have some fabulous material. The short stories are better than any you see in the weekend papers here. I love the one about the incompetent sailor and his wife."

"It's not a very serious one – just there really to show I can do a bit of humour."

"Of course you can – and also the human dramas. You are very good about marriages – and I know why."

We laughed knowingly at that. I had by then

told her the full story of my marriage breakup and had made comedy of my enforced bachelor status.

"Bernie – you know, the publisher I told you about - well he had a quick look at the novel – I twisted his arm a bit, they're so awful at getting things done – and he says it will need some editing, but what he read looks promising. Isn't that wonderful? If he thinks it's good we'll be able to get you signed up with one of the New York agencies and you can kiss goodbye to your hopeless English one. You deserve to do better darling. I'm so excited that he likes it."

"That is really fantastic. You are a star. I can't wait to be with you there. Please, please push them to set something up quickly so I have a good reason to come over."

"Oh I will darling. I've even chosen the hotel we are going to stay in. Discreet, small, mid-town – you'll love it. Cocktails at seven, dinner in my favourite Italian – it's going to be wonderful. And you – wowing the agents – they're going to love your accent and the whole story about you sitting writing on the yacht. Good profile material."

At the end of the conversation we went on to more mundane matters.

"Darling, I've been talking to Vernon – I hope you don't mind?"

"Of course not." I was buzzing with the prospect not only of interested agents and publishers, but also the anticipation of that tanned, knowing body.

"He's furious with your broker. Says you should sack him immediately. He doesn't usually take on small individual clients, but darling I know I could persuade him if you wanted me to."

"Of course, that would be wonderful."

"I'll talk to him tomorrow. I'll get him to email the forms for you to fill in. He's awfully organised."

We exchanged loving noises and silences. Then she was gone.

Sure enough Vernon emailed the forms and I quickly filled in the details and signed the authority for him to manage my dwindling but still substantial holdings.

January came and went. Veronica was profusely apologetic about the slowness of her literary friends. 'You know what they are like.' And indeed I did. Our mutual longing for a physical meeting seemed to be fuelled by our separation, and the phone calls were at times adolescent in their explicit impropriety.

During February Veronica was more positive about the prospect of meetings. Her best friend's husband had been at their house for dinner and promised to read my pieces.

March and April were disappointingly similar. Scraps of positive interest faded to disappointment.

On the positive side Vernon was being as good as his word. Each month I received an elaborate statement analysing my investment by sector, by geography and by volatility. Coloured charts compared the performance to market benchmarks and basically it was going extremely well. The monthly growth was promising an annual return well over 10%, maybe as much as twice that. I thanked my guardian angel for that chance meeting on the Turkish coast.

On 9th June at 10:15 I received a phone call.

"Is that Mr Drummond? Detective Inspector Crane here. Could you confirm you first names please?"

I did so, with an ominous feeling in the pit of my stomach.

"Just for the record, sir, can you confirm your date of birth and postal address?"

I completed the required litany to his satisfaction, but with the increasing pangs of anxiety that unexpected dealings with the police are guaranteed to elicit.

"I'd like to pop around to see you if that's alright?"

"Of course, but what's this all about."

"I'll explain everything when I see you. Eleven o'clock OK?"

"Yes, yes, fine. I'll be here."

I tried to think of anything remotely improper that I had been involved in. With a sinking feeling I guessed that something unpleasant had surfaced from my old company days. I thought of the female employees who might have belatedly made some sort of complaint about my behaviour. It had always lurked at the back of my mind that although they had been willing partners at the time, a couple of them could concoct a harassment case that I'd have difficulty disproving. I tried to imagine which of them it might be. I knew that I didn't have any of the passionate notes one or two had sent me – all shredded years ago – so it would be my word against theirs. I wondered about the legalities. How long after the supposed offence could a complaint be made? I remembered the high-profile cases of celebrities whose misdeeds a lifetime ago seemed to be still eligible legally.

I have to admit I sweated those forty-five

minutes. I checked that I had my solicitor's number handy, but didn't ring yet – what would I say? I thought about how I was going to handle it with my ex-wife. How could I break it in a way that didn't ruin the fragile cooperation we had managed to construct? The children: how could I face them when this all came out?

I tried to prepare a tray with coffee and biscuits, but shaking hands rattled the cups so much that I decided not to bother.

At 11:05 the doorbell rang. I took a deep breath and forced myself to walk normally down the parquet floor to open the door.

Detective Inspector Crane was a mild looking man in his late forties. He looked more like an accountant than a hard-bitten detective from television. He had with him a younger constable, a female, whose name I forget. I settled them in the living room, conscious of appraising eyes taking in the recently bought furniture; the high ceilings; the contemporary art on the walls; the Linn hi-fi; and sensed the accountant's judgement about my financial status.

"Mr Drummond, I'm afraid you are not going to like what I have to say."

I hadn't expected to like it, but this sounded like a truly ominous opening.

"You'll have heard of Bernie Madoff, Mr Drummond, and I suppose we all thought we'd seen the last of that sort of financial scam…"

The rest of his sentence was blocked out by a sudden thundering in my ears. I experienced a dizzy lurch, and I'm sure the detectives must have seen me blanche. In an instant I saw it all. It was all there waiting for me to piece together and see how it had been done. The brain seems to be able to work fast even when the body is virtually paralysed with shock. I recreated each little scene from the Turkish bay to the enthusing over my writing, and the fabrication of the agents, publishers, contacts and friends.

"I'm sorry, could you repeat that please. I didn't quite take it in."

The Tribe

Once upon a time there was a tribe living in the impenetrable forest in deepest, most unexplored, South America. In the early 2000s, when money was plentiful, an exploration was attempted. A key part of the exercise was to drop an expedition vehicle by helicopter onto the high plateau, as there was no possible access up the steep cliffs and closely packed trees.

    The Land Rover, with its balloon tyres and water-protected engine, was dropped in a clearing near the top of a very recognisable ravine. The intention was to try to send the ground party up the ravine, and to drop more supplies when they were in place. Unfortunately the financial crisis struck. The university mounting the expedition had to cut its spending, and the expensive project was the first thing to go.

The cost of the Land Rover and the helicopter drop was written off, while the other equipment was sold or stored for better times.

Meanwhile, the tribe on the high plateau lived on in blissful isolation. They had lived for as long as any of them could remember in the very centre of the plateau – which was several hundreds of miles in diameter. Their home was self-sufficient in food and water. The ground was naturally fertile, and the semi-tropical location blessed them with plentiful rainfall.

Agriculture was simple but effective. There was little mechanisation, but tools made from wood, from flints, and from the simple iron castings they could create, and were adequate for the task. They had developed to something approximating to our middle ages, but in some ways they were more primitive, while in other ways surprisingly advanced. Their use of fire had led them to develop metal smelting, but the limited types of ore available to them meant that iron and copper were their main products. Gold and silver were almost disdained as plentiful but too soft for much practical work. They developed a steel-making process similar to ancient Chinese methods which were laborious, inefficient and time-consuming, but they had no access to light metals like aluminium.

Their shelters were mainly wood and mud, and the plentiful creepers in the forests gave them the materials for strong ropes and cord. Overall they would have looked to the university expedition, had they ever arrived, as a stable and functioning pre-industrial civilisation, with relatively sophisticated family and social organisation, a surprisingly advanced grasp of practical science, and a notable lack of threat either from the environment, from human enemies, or from predators.

The use of agriculture was in line with parallel developments in the documented history of our world, perhaps hastened by the limited horizons of their high domain, and the bountiful provision of plant and animal food. Their natural organisational ability led them to corral and tame the animals, and to plant the vegetables they needed within easy reach. It would have seemed to the planned expedition to be a prototypical Garden of Eden – with no sign of the mischievous snake.

The people of the tribe – both male and female – fell into two opposing camps. One group was very content with the way things were. They worshipped a sky-god, whom they credited with the provision of the food and natural resources in their world, and they regarded their god as the guarantor of their continuing stability and happiness.

The opposing group were sceptical about the sky-god. They discounted the myths about a long-ago visitation from the sky-god, noisily distributing mysterious bounty, and sought simple common-sense explanations for the phenomena they experienced. Crop failures were due to disease or flaws in their husbandry rather than punishments from above. Sicknesses were puzzles to solve and deal with in a rational and scientific way.

Systematic explorations to the limits of their world formed a key part of their national folklore. It was as if they periodically needed to reassure themselves that there was indeed an impenetrable barrier that circumscribed their existence. The dizzying cliffs had never been scaled, and formed part of the mythology of frightening perils that lay beneath the constant clouds.

The most recent expedition consisted of three parties, each responsible for a pie-slice of the plateau. Laden with enough food for a month's trek, they all set off with feelings of duty rather than expectation.

Two groups returned within the allotted month. Of the third group there was no sign. The first groups reported no change to the limits of their world. No new threats or opportunities had presented themselves.

Anxiety increased day by day as the third group failed to appear. At last, a week later, a runner arrived at the centre full of news about an amazing discovery and requesting volunteers to return to help group three carry the most amazing discovery.

Twenty strong runners were dispatched to meet the struggling party, and three days later a noisy parade entered town carrying on a wooden platform a greenly deteriorated Land Rover. Forest conditions had covered the windows and metal with a layer of green algae that made the vehicle look as if it had grown naturally in the forest. No shine or transparency betrayed the true nature of the find, but it was unlike anything ever encountered by the tribe.

Days of tentative rubbing and poking gradually began to reveal the glass and metal surfaces. The tribe was well used to the growth of mould and algae in their hot and humid environment, and intuitively understood that the strange object had not always looked as they had found it.

The theists announced that at last they had proof positive of an external being – something that was capable of producing an artefact of complexity and function that was not of their world, and thus demonstrably proof of existence and intelligence beyond their known world.

The scientists disagreed. They began to systematically analyse and dismantle the Land Rover. They were first most taken with the glass windows, as their experiments with fire had not led them down that path. Having thoroughly examined the bodywork, they concluded that it was not in fact dissimilar to the metals that they were creating in the town smelter. Granted it was lighter and finer than anything they could yet produce, but it was recognisably of the same nature.

The tyres were at first puzzling, for they were flat and airless when they found the vehicle. The wheel had of course been developed before any of their remembered history, and methods of helping it run smoothly on hard surfaces had been developed, but pneumatic inflation had not yet been thought of. It took a bright young scientist to hit on the concept of inflating the rubber tyres, and she was able to draw convincing diagrams of how beneficial this would be to the operation of the wheels. Eventually a modified bellows from the smelter was able to partially inflate one of the tyres and prove the point.

Having progressed beyond the external features of the Land Rover, they came to the engine and running gear. What infinite delight the scientists took in the way that random aggregations of metal elements could come together to produce a creation of such order and complexity. Their experiments included the filing off of samples of the metal engine block, which they were able to melt and mould into other shapes – demonstrating that what they had was another manifestation of their known world rather than anything requiring a creative god.

The theists were as adamant in the contrary view. Each piece of discovery was used by them to illustrate the wonder of the creative genius behind the Land Rover. They were baffled at the stance of the scientists who insisted that there were natural explanations for all of these wonders.

One day the scientists announced that they had uncovered the very core of the object. They most celebrated and talented technicians had dismantled the engine and gearbox, uncovering beauty and refinement beyond their wildest dreams. Metal pieces in the cog-box, as they named it, had taken on an external form that meshed perfectly with other matching pieces. The wonders of nature enthused them endlessly. However it was a mighty leap of insight that enabled them to see that the system of pipes and valves introduced an explosive vapour into each of the internal containers, and that the moving cores could be impelled by the explosion of the vapour. This insight led them to very grand claims of having uncovered the very secrets of the Land Rover's existence.

The great experiment, years in the making, was to settle the matter once and for all. It was hailed as demonstrating through the tribe's technology that the mystery vehicle was in fact understandable and subject to the same laws of nature as they were. No metaphysical explanations were needed. Science was gradually extending the tribe's understanding, and the more they uncovered, the more sure they were of the supremacy of their view of the world.

A metal tube had been constructed, with a sliding core. The demonstration of the 'Contained Explosion Principle' was billed as the final nail in the coffin of the theists.

"If we can demonstrate this, the door is open to explaining every aspect of the mystery construction."

And the experiment was a success. An explosive vapour was introduced into the sealed tube, the moving core was pressed home, the vapour was compressed with a complex system of levers and pulleys. Finally a flint-strike within the tube ignited the vapour. The moving core shot out of the tube with a force even the scientists had not predicted, killing several bystanders and terrifying the observers.

"It is with a sense of awe and humility that we conclude this experiment," intoned the chief scientist. "Those who have given their lives in the advancement of science will always be remembered, and their work will not be in vain. We have finally laid to rest the myths and superstition that have held back this tribe. What the theists see as mysteries and as evidence of other intelligences has been demonstrated to be within the realm of our understanding and capable of rational explanation. Today is truly the first day of a glorious flowering of our understanding of the universe, and a step towards our inevitable management of it."

A brave theist stepped forward.

"You have explained one tiny fraction of how this wondrous construction works, but have given no explanation of how it came to be, nor of why it came to be. Don't you see the limitation of your view? Can't you see that some intelligent being must have designed the thing, and must have had some reason for creating it?"

The scientists laughed, and shook their heads in disdain.

Life: disrupted

Part 1

I leapt off the moving bus at the foot of Asylum Road, and with a slightly unnerving slip of the left foot made it to the footpath. The sound of a 1964 Commer van horn was ringing in my ears.

"That was close," I thought to myself, as I waved supposedly nonchalantly to the bus conductor, who stood on the open rear platform of the bus, one eyebrow raised, shaking his head sorrowfully.

I had to leave the bus abruptly because I urgently needed to meet Kathy, the girl with the strawberry blond hair, who was walking purposefully towards the steps of the Technical College. I had been watching anxiously for her, but only caught a glimpse of the unmistakable hair at the last minute, so had to risk life and limb to manufacture a casual encounter.

Come to think of it, her hair couldn't have been the main thing I had recognised, because most of it was bunched up and stuck under one of those oversized bulbous caps that were fashionable at the time. If it wasn't just her hair, it must have been her general movement and body-size, for it was all wrapped up in a jacket and skirt that I hadn't seen before.

"Hi Kathy," I managed to splutter in a very unsophisticated breathless outburst. To my intense relief she immediately paused, turned, and with that quizzical tilt of her head, smiled and said,

"Yes."

That may sound like a strange response, but in the Derry/Londonderry of the 1960s it was, and may still be, the local equivalent of 'hi'.

What a simple word. But how utterly, earth-shatteringly, delightfully, completely, and life-changingly significant it was. Different schools, different backgrounds, and what is quaintly referred to as different 'religious affiliation', meant that our paths had not crossed in the normal course of events.

Not until the previous Saturday night 'hop' in the Society Hall off Bishop Street. I had spent many a fruitless night there, listening to the local bands and attempting to chat up the girls from the High School. Naturally there had been a good few adolescently passionate kisses and fumbles with the well-brought-up girls, but we were all so familiar with each other it seemed almost incestuous in retrospect.

I asked Kathy to dance, because I couldn't take my eyes off her. Her hair was less conservatively groomed than the High School girls', her tartan skirt a little more daring, her blouse discreetly displaying the outline of the most perfect breasts I had ever seen, but it was more than any of those – more the confidently challenging message encoded in the way she moved; the forthright look from her big, big eyes – (in the dim light of the hop I couldn't even discern the delectable greenish hazel shade); the fact that she was unmistakably different.

"Yes," I said amiably. It was as if that strange Derry greeting was for once a real answer to a hundred life-defining questions that had yet to be formed, but in time would be construed, posed, answered and welcomed, in the forbidden, disapproved, risky, and unavoidable romance that followed. A romance that would lead to a life, a family, and a feeling of belonging that would give a warm glow to the greyest day.

However that bus-leaping day was the first encounter after the weekend's dance. I didn't know how she would react. Was I an interesting experiment that obviously couldn't go anywhere? Did she regret the kisses, the soft words, and the tentative but chaste exploration of her delectable body?

The smile told me that all was well. I saw the relaxation in her stance; the fractional movement towards me; the willingness to pause and continue where we had left off.

"Nice to see you," I managed. "I really enjoyed Saturday night."

"I'm glad. So did I."

"Bit unexpected."

"And why would you not expect to enjoy walking me home?"

"I mean…"

She laughed. She knew. I hadn't ever walked a girl home to one of the streets on the City side. It was always one of the leafy roads on the Waterside, or out towards Culmore. She knew, and enjoyed the momentary squirm she caused.

"I'm really glad you enjoyed it. Sorry for tweaking your sensitivities." But she said it with such warmth in the boldness that I felt OK.

"I'd really like to do it again," I tried.

"Want to meet up after this?" she asked, indicating the Technical College with an inclination of her head.

"Great. A coffee or something?"

"Probably just a something. See you back at Asylum Road about 4?"

She was so sensible! Standing on the steps waiting for her I'd have felt a right dick. For her to stand there outside the college would have been impossibly public. A hundred yards away and round the corner was far better. I loved her absolutely.

Part 2

The Commer van driver was checking his delivery dockets. He couldn't remember where the next drop-off was, so his eyes had left the road after the school bus had safely pulled away. Although he rationalised it later, and told the police there just wasn't time to swerve or brake, the truth was that the first he knew of it was the noise and the feeling of the van hitting a human body.

The driver cursed, felt sick, and experienced a wave of horror as immediately after the initial impact he felt the van bump and lurch over the body he had hit. He was distantly aware of a shout, which was followed by a scream and the sound of running feet. He felt faint, unable to move, unsure if he was going to be sick.

The bus conductor had helplessly watched as, despite his shouted warning, the schoolboy had jumped from the platform of the moving bus. He might have been safe if he hadn't slipped and needed to pause to regain his balance. The van didn't swerve or brake. The conductor knew that the driver was not looking up. When he replayed the scene in his mind's eye, as he was doomed to continue doing for years, he could see the top of the driver's head as he looked down at something inside the van rather than at the road ahead.

Someone dialled 999 from the phone box at the street corner. The white-coated pharmacist from the Chemist's shop ran out into the road to tend the schoolboy. A girl from the Technical College screamed, and now stood, hands to her face, deathly pale as she stared, transfixed, at the boy on the road.

A pool of blood was forming around the maroon blazer and the grey flannels. The clothing hid the injuries to some extent, but the unnatural angle of the limbs and the bloodied mess of the head left no doubt about the seriousness.

The pharmacist's white coat was stained red on the sleeves and the neatly pressed front, as he gingerly tried to ascertain if there was anything he could do. Even his professional eye could scarcely bring itself to examine the boy's head. He felt for a pulse at the available wrist and knew there was still life. He heard the distant siren of the ambulance and prayed they would arrive and relieve him of his unwanted role.

The circle of onlookers grew and had to be marshalled by the natural organisers who emerged from the crowd. Someone diverted traffic up Asylum Road, another admonished the circling crowd and called for space to let the ambulance through.

The ambulance men brought a stretcher but looked dubious about how to proceed. A doctor at last arrived from his surgery in nearby Clarendon Street, carrying his leather bag and wearing a purposeful frown. He knelt with the ambulance men and took stock of the twisted body with its dark pool of ebbing blood. The spine was certainly gone he could see. The internal damage would be enormous. The boy's eyes were open but sightless and he could detect no sign of breath. He followed the pharmacist's instinctive check of pulse at the wrist, and finding none, felt for the jugular.

He shook his head, and the ambulance men

spread the dark grey blanket over the body. The girl fainted, and someone shouted for the doctor to come to her aid.

A lecturer from the College recognised her and knelt as the doctor rolled her into the recovery position and checked her breathing.

"Kathy, Kathy, it's alright. We'll get you inside in a minute. It's alright. You're alright."

The girl came round and her eyelids flickered.

"You're alright. You're alright."

Her consciousness returned and she put together what had happened. As the horror returned, she felt as if her whole life, her future, the new-found joy and excitement had been snatched away in the fatal moment. Her knees came up to her chin as she curled into a hopeless, inconsolable wail. She shook her head to dismiss the well-meant but totally erroneous reassurance.

The Accident

"What do you think, darling?"

"I really don't know. Whatever suits you, dear."

"But you must have a preference."

"No, really. You can decide. If I say something it will be wrong anyway."

"Why do you say that?"

"It's just because you know best, and I'm really happy with whatever you decide."

"That's not helpful. And I don't like you suggesting that I bully you."

"I'm sorry."

"Please stop saying you're sorry for everything. There's nothing to be sorry for, except that I can't get a straight answer out of you."

"But you know what the forecasts are, and you know what your overall plan is, so you are in a better position to make the decision."

"This is supposed to be joint decision making. I want your opinion and I'm really tired of the insinuation that you have to do what I want."

"I'm sorry. I didn't mean…."

"There you go again. 'I'm sorry.' Just bloody well stop being sorry for everything and have an intelligent adult discussion."

"I'm …. I'm doing my best. But if I make a suggestion you'll ask me why, and I won't have a good technical reason for it."

"You make me sound like a tyrant."

"I'm … I'm only explaining why I'm happier to let you make the decision."

"This is really typical of life isn't it? Total failure to communicate."

"That isn't fair."

"But it's the truth. We tiptoe around each other, afraid of giving offence or causing a row. All I want to do is decide if we stay another night here or sail across the gulf to the bays on the other side."

"And I'm just pointing out that I'm happy with either, so it's best if you decide."

Tim cursed under his breath and went down the companionway to the chart table. He slammed the dividers on the open chart and clenched his fists in frustrated rage. He didn't look at the chart, nor at the forecasts that he had noted earlier. He closed his eyes and tried to calm himself. Deep breaths. Deep breaths. Count to ten. No count to twenty. Counting to a thousand wouldn't make any fucking difference.

"OK," he shouted up to the cockpit, "we'll stay another night here and make the long trip tomorrow."

"That's lovely dear. Whatever you think."

Tim flinched at the words and turned to shout something hurtful back, but managed to restrain himself. With rough and unnecessarily noisy movements he sorted through the charts and tried to focus on planning a course for the following day. His concentration was hopeless. The frustration with Barbara kept flaring into an impotent rage at the woman. How had he allowed himself to get into such a relationship?

Barbara was Tim's second marriage. His first had broken down acrimoniously some years earlier, when his wife had eagerly seized on the evidence of Tim's unfaithfulness to bring an end to their ten childless years. 'Mental cruelty and unfaithfulness' had been the reasons cited in the papers. His solicitor had advised against fighting it, so Tim had found himself living as a single man again.

Barbara on the other hand had never married. She was approaching her fortieth with anxiety and a deep sense of failure. She was attractive but not classically beautiful. She was a constant source of puzzlement to her friends. 'Just didn't find the right man at the right time,' they concluded. 'Too picky,' was also suggested. Her closest friends finally persuaded her to try internet dating.

It had been one of their 'girls' nights out'. All the others were married, most with children, and they had agreed that Barbara was a problem to be solved.

"I mean, 'late thirties – well we'll say early, or maybe mid? – Attractive, intelligent, successful professional woman, seeks relationship with similar male.' What do you think girls?"

"GSOH – they all say GSOH."

"Good Set of Hands?"

They all laughed uproariously. Barbara blushed and half hoped they would persuade her and half hoped they wouldn't. She had enjoyed a few good relationships in her teens and twenties, but somehow none had felt quite right, and besides there was the job to concentrate on. She had studied literature at university, because she enjoyed it rather than because she had a career plan. She graduated well, and knowing that she did not want to teach, jumped at the welcoming home the Civil Service offered her. Not that she was blue-stocking old maid material. She saw herself as one of the new generation of successful civil servants, and had made rapid progress, partly through luck, and partly because of her impressive academic record.

Having reached a senior post in a Whitehall department by her mid thirties, she was comfortably well off, and enjoyed her ability to afford a Pimlico apartment.

Tim was what the red-tops called a 'self-made man', an 'entrepreneur', or a 'tycoon', depending on the style of the journalist. He was at heart a wheeler-dealer. His first business in the 90s had been in business computerisation. He recognised that everyone was to some extent in the dark about what was possible and what worked. There were competing packages for accounting and office information that all ran on the ubiquitous Microsoft platform. He gathered a few old friends from his computer studies course and they majored on slick sales techniques. They built up a respectable client base in a couple of years, and knew as much as most about what they were doing. Tim had an eye for PR, and the company publicity materials were worthy of a company many times larger. It was largely this successful image building that allowed him to sell the company to a larger organisation and pocket his first significant fortune.

His next venture was in computerising retail businesses, and he again quickly built a reputation as an innovator in EPOS applications. In fact he was a wheeler-dealer with products whose originators lacked his PR flair, and with a customer base who knew they needed to do something but weren't sure what.

Having sold the second business he saw the year 2000 hysteria building and made another fortune selling consultancy and new computers to people who didn't really need them. Once that bubble had burst he moved on to web-based systems, and built a solid little consultancy business with some recent graduates who really did know what they were doing.

By this stage his fortune was made and he enjoyed playing the successful CEO – speaking at conferences and advising young entrepreneurs. "When you see the opportunity – grab it – don't hesitate," was his mantra.

His marriage to Fiona was built on his image as a successful and admirable businessman. The image cracked relatively quickly when she discovered that the entrepreneur's obvious confidence came with the unwelcome trimmings of a bullying nature, and an inclination to take chances of a less business-like nature when they presented themselves – which they did quite frequently as he was a good-looking and slick-talking seducer.

Fiona never quite understood that the marriage was part of the image-building process rather than an affair of the heart. Her upper class connections and accent were a balance to his chance-taking nature, and helped build the solid, successful persona that worked wonders with clients, government officials and susceptible women. He genuinely believed that if he bought Fiona enough expensive presents and allowed her to spend freely on her credit cards, she would overlook, in fact she had no business questioning, his extra-marital affairs. It was a blow to his view of the world when she called his bluff and settled for a considerable chunk of his declared fortune. Luckily she knew nothing about the rest of it.

So Tim was newly on the legitimate 'loose' when he met Barbara at a Business and Innovation conference. She was his government liaison, and she was thoroughly enthralled by the smooth-talking, Armani suited exemplar. He suggested drinks after the conference, and was intrigued by Barbara's obvious interest in him but refusal to jump into bed.

It was probably this refusal that led him into actually courting her. He couldn't cope with defeat. For their different reasons they blundered on into a disastrous marriage - she, so that she could tell the girls that internet dating was not required, - he, so that he was not defeated in an attempted conquest.

The honeymoon was in Barbados, not because there was anything there that they wanted to do or see, but because Tim thought it 'sounded right'. They managed to avoid confronting their fundamental incompatibility under the cover of 'adjusting,' and 'learning about each other'. When Barbara came to admit to herself what a self-centred shallow bully he was, she was perplexed. She couldn't face admitting it was a mistake – not after all these years of being pitied for being single. When Tim realised what an able, and principled person she was, and how different she was in every way from him, he wanted out, but he hated the stigma of another failure.

So they plodded on, most of the time being excessively polite to each other. Flare-ups gradually became more frequent, and it was more and more obvious that Barbara had the measure of him, and was tightening her supervision of his extra-mural activities. Too polite to confront him, she ensured that she accompanied him to conferences, and gave him less and less scope for – for what? – 'for life for goodness sake – to enjoy myself – not to sit around and read a book, or discuss the fucking Booker Prize shortlist.'

In this simmering mess of disguised discord Tim proposed a holiday that he had always wanted to try, and while he would prefer a willing companion, he didn't much care if Barbara liked the idea or not. He chartered a yacht in Turkey for two weeks, and convinced himself and the charter company that he was sufficiently competent to be allowed the boat.

He wasn't actually as competent as he thought, and there were a few embarrassing events when marina staff had to take over in order to dock the boat successfully. They 'sailed', or rather motored, from bay to bay, partly following the itinerary suggested by the charter company but extended by the self-confident Tim.

When faced with the decision to stay or take

the long journey from the peninsula west of Marmaris right across fifty miles of open sea to the Gulf of Fethiye, Barbara's comment that 'you know best' was possibly not without a hint of sarcasm. Stung by his public embarrassments in failing to dock the boat competently, Tim was sensitive and ready to take offence. The more he dwelt on her reaction, and on what he saw as her mocking submissiveness, the more his aversion and dislike turned to a festering hatred.

They spent the evening almost entirely silently. Barbara read her book, went with Tim to the taverna where they exchanged a few comments on the food, and then returned to her cabin to read her book. It had become 'her cabin' when Tim had announced that it was too cramped for the two of them, and he moved into one of the spare cabins. He had of course chartered a yacht that was much larger than necessary. His self-deception about his level of competence blinded him to the fact that the larger yacht would actually be harder for him to manage, and would expose his failings more dramatically.

They prepared for departure the following morning in a tense atmosphere. Tim was slightly nervous by now about handling the large yacht and knew that each landfall and docking exercise was a test he was sure to fail. This led him to be more demanding and sharp in his instructions to his crew.

They set off at 8:00 a.m. and after three hours of increasingly hot sun Barbara suggested that erecting the bimini sunshade over the cockpit would be a good idea. The polite Tim of months earlier would probably have said, 'of course dear, I'll do that', but the frustrated Tim said,

"Whatever you want. I've shown you how to do it so suit yourself."

With remarkable good grace Barbara unzipped the canvas canopy and swung the metal frame forward to stretch and support the bimini over the cockpit. She had to step up onto the side-deck to secure the straps that held the frame in place and made the canvas taut.

Tim watched, ready to criticise or mock her efforts. But Barbara knew what she was doing as she balanced on the narrow deck to finish the task. She stood a little unsteadily, working at the buckle on the strap, protected from the sea only by the safety wires that stretched along each side of the yacht between the stanchions. They came to around knee height for anyone standing on the side deck - not something the charter company recommended for anyone without a life-jacket.

Barbara wobbled unsteadily as she stood to return to the cockpit. In some sort of unpremeditated grasping of an opportunity Tim swung the wheel violently to starboard. With a brief shriek Barbara disappeared over the side.

'Don't look back,' Tim told himself. He gripped the wheel tightly and stared rigidly at the distant horizon. 'You can't go back now. She knows what you did. You can't pick her up after that. Don't look back. It's done now.'

He felt a mixture of panic and elation at what he had done. It was unlike anything he had ever done before. Nasty business practices were one thing – but killing someone? He corrected himself. He failed to rescue her – which was different from killing her. It was a tragic accident.

Tim turned his mind to managing the situation. Barbara was a poor swimmer, and she wasn't wearing a life-jacket. She could manage no more than a few strokes. Even if he turned back now it would be no use. But he knew he couldn't just turn up in Fethiye with Barbara missing. Unless he destroyed her passport and disposed of her clothes? He could say that they had argued and she had left him at one of the earlier ports. He dismissed that idea as they had been seen leaving Loryma that morning.

One hour later, and six miles further towards Fethiye Tim slowed the yacht and began slowly circling. He picked up the radio microphone, "Mayday, Mayday, Mayday. This is yacht October, yacht October. Man overboard. Man overboard. My position is 36°35'N, 28°35'E. Please help. Man overboard."

Six miles behind, on a yacht crewed by a group of friendly and competent Englishmen, Barbara was sitting wrapped in a blanket and sipping a brandy. The Mayday message came through on the radio.

"Quick," she begged, "an iPhone. Record that message and me sitting here." As Tim dutifully repeated the Mayday call, the iPhone recorded the message and the recovering Barbara. Then the skipper turned the camera towards himself and said,

"This is the 'man overboard' we rescued 45 minutes ago at position 36°35'N, 28°29'E. There seems to be some confusion here."

Barbara was not a strong swimmer, but she had reserves of calm collectedness that served her well at work, and even more so at moments of crisis. She knew that she could float successfully, particularly if she relaxed and kept plenty of air in her lungs. She also knew that the route they were on was a well-travelled one. A number of other yachts were planning the same route from Loryma to Fethiye, and there would be many going the other direction. She was lucky. The sea was flat calm. Waves did not overwhelm her, and she lay on her back, breathing in a controlled way, listening and watching for rescue. When the English yacht came along the well-travelled highway she waved and shouted. She didn't need to. They had already spotted her and were coming straight to her rescue.

The English skipper had earlier reported the rescue to the Coastguard. While he spoke to the Coastguard again, Barbara quietly imagined the reception that her husband was about to experience in Fethiye. Her tight little smile was grim and her intentions merciless.

Julia

"I'm sorry Jimmy. I thought you knew this was coming."

"How would I have known? You told me three weeks ago my job was safe."

"I had to keep things under wraps – you know that."

"So tell me again what the score is."

"We didn't match the price of the Chinese for the seat belt contract. Without that we just can't keep going. They're running down production of the door fittings and luggage blinds, just to see out the existing contracts, then production will all go elsewhere."

"Just like that? Fifteen years of work written off without a second thought? And I suppose you have a nice job somewhere else in the group?"

"No need to be bitter. I'd have thought that you of all people would have seen the inevitability of this. As it happens I do have the offer of a move to

HQ but I don't know yet if I'll take it. I really did try to find something for you, but the main accountancy department is slimming down just like everywhere else, and all we can do is the package that's on the table."

"Three month's pay in lieu of notice, and statutory redundancy – that's it? How am I supposed to survive on that? The chances of another job are pretty slim."

"Look you're only fifty-three, healthy and well qualified, you'll be fine."

"Easy for you to say," muttered James numbly.

"For goodness sake Jimmy, you're the most organised, sensible, and analytical person I know. You just have to apply those skills to the job hunt."

James had worked for the subsidiary of a major car manufacturer, one of the flexible 'semi-outsourced' suppliers of seat-belts, mouldings, and other ancillary bits and pieces that in the end could be bought from any one of a number of suppliers. The nasty reality of business was that the factory kept its position as supplier only as long as it was as cheap as any of the other competing manufacturers. When the downturn hit the car industry it was almost inevitable that James' company would close.

He began to get up later each morning. He didn't sleep well. When he went to bed, usually after the 10:00 o'clock news, he could fall asleep much as usual, but found that he was waking again just a few hours later. Night after night he watched the green digital display on the bedside clock make its cruelly slow progress from hour to hour. He willed the coming of dawn and the hour when it was reasonable to get up and make some breakfast, but more and more frequently he was falling into a mis-timed sleep around 7:00 a.m., and waking again about 9:00, annoyed with himself for sleeping in; dissatisfied with his night's sleep; feeling tired and lethargic. He knew that he should be doing something about physical exercise, but somehow couldn't find the energy to actually get started. The failure left him feeling more negative about himself, and irrationally less able to take the simple practical action. He saw the flabbiness of his belly, felt heavier and suddenly older, but was frustratingly incapable of responding.

After a month he stopped looking at the job advertisements. How could he survive on a part time job as an accounts administrator? By the time he paid the travel costs and lost his benefit he'd be worse off than sitting at home. He was damned if he would let neighbours see him stacking shelves in the supermarket, but at the same time knew he wasn't the sort of person they wanted for the job in any case. He gave up ringing the employment agency that had set up temporary offices in the old factory. He stopped thinking in terms of his next job. He no longer believed there would be one.

James couldn't pin down the deeper dissatisfaction and frustration that he felt. He had never articulated a particular ambition that he was driven to achieve. His feeling of failure was not based on the frustration of a specific goal. That might have been easier to deal with; to articulate; or to rage over. His goals had never been consciously formulated in his mind, but the absence of decently paid work; the absence of an externally imposed structure and rhythm to his day; the absence of the 'credit' item from his monthly bank statement; by their absence defined what his modest goals and ambitions had been.

"Don't worry dear, I'm sure you'll find something," his wife had vaguely offered. Freda was distantly concerned for his joblessness, but she had always been thoroughly engrossed in her own library job, the WI, and the Oxfam shop. She had never been interested in the detail of his world, had never sought to understand his worries and problems.

"How am I supposed to find something when every worthwhile company seems to be closing down and the only jobs around are part-time and pathetic?"

"Well talk to those people in the factory. There must be something for a man like you. But you'll have the pension anyway so you really don't need to worry."

"How many times have I told you the pension scheme was closed five years ago when it became too expensive? What I paid in will amount to peanuts when I'm sixty. There's nothing in the meantime."

"Oh I'm sure you have your savings sorted. I know you. By the way I'm out tonight, WI dinner, you'll have to look after yourself." Her tweedy bulk bustled round the kitchen, gathering bulging plastic bags from the floor and sticky notes from the noticeboard.

James had never been demonstrative or wordy about his marriage. James and Freda. Everyone thought of them as a well-matched couple, but now he scarcely spoke to her. Childless. A cold and disheartening word. Barren. Depressing. He found no comfort or compensation in their relationship. Freda's weight, wrinkles and style-less-ness had removed her further and further from any approximation of a sexual fantasy. Even before his redundancy they had reached the stage where James could not reliably remember the last time they had sex. Pointless. Stultifying. Unfulfilling. These were not part of James' normal vocabulary. Perhaps they should have been. Apparently it is helpful to express these things. He found depression was not selective, and realised eventually that he had come to feel that every aspect of life was pointless.

Suicides are a strange phenomenon. It is quite rare for family and friends to say, 'Yes, we saw that coming.' More common is an expression of disbelief - the quoting of activities or plans that were quite counter to the intent to end a life. The absence of threat or declaration of purpose is common in many successful suicides.

Even stranger is the extent to which human beings can maintain conflicting realities. It is possible to continue with activities and plans for the day; for tomorrow; even for the coming summer; while the dark, depressed, defeated part of the self is planning and organising its end.

James had decided that the irony of using his car would be blackly appropriate. He had read enough newspaper reports to know that carbon monoxide poisoning was easy to arrange and not a bad way to go. Hosepipes and other apparatus were quite unnecessary as their secluded and well-sealed garage was perfect for the process. He hadn't picked the day, but had calculated that keeping the garage doors firmly closed, and sitting in the car with windows open, engine idling, the fumes would have done their work hours before Freda returned from her job at the library.

But not today. Instead he had the mundane necessity of going to the shops to buy something for his evening meal.

As he wearily and indecisively plodded round the aisles, picking up an instant pasta, and immediately dumping it for a tin of curry, he crossed paths with the same people on each parade down the aisles. One shopper seemed to stand out from the shuffling crowd. She was tall, athletic-looking, and attractive in a healthy out-door way. She had the first hints of grey in her cropped blond hair, and looked as if she was in her thirties, but more likely ten years older. She was carrying a basket rather than pushing a trolley – the certain sign of a single shopper. Wearing a loose grey tracksuit with a bright blue oriental scarf, she looked more relaxed and physically confident than the other shoppers. She somehow made the tracksuit look stylish. James didn't know why, but they smiled at each other. It was not something he had done for weeks. Something irrational but irresistible stirred in James, and he ensured that he was exiting from the shop at the same time as the attractive female.

Diffidently he almost smiled as they walked to the car park. Short fair hair brushed back from her face; a fading tan; an open enquiring look on her lightly freckled face; she touched some receptive part of his mind and sparked a long-forgotten emotional response. His pulse quickened. He held himself more erect and walked with a more confident gait. He found the spontaneous attraction as irresistible as it was ridiculous.

But she was responding. That unmistakable spark of interest in the eyes; the subtle but significant physical movement towards rather than away from him; the provocative and alluring tilt of her head as they exchanged mundane comments about the day.

"You shop here regularly?" She asked.

"Yes, it's the nearest to home."

"It seems quite, how do you say, comprehensive?"

"Yes, I think it is probably the best one. Are you new here?"

"Yes, not long. I have an apartment by the river."

"Working here?"

"Yes, in the university. And you?"

"In between I'm afraid."

"Oh I'm sorry. Maybe we can talk sometime?"

"I'd like that."

"I must be in a hurry today but perhaps next time we could have coffee?"

She shook his hand in that formal German way and with a slight nod of the head said, "Julia."

He smiled, felt the warmth in her hand, the promise in her eyes, and said, "James."

His organised habits quickly dealt with the exchange of phone numbers, the checking of dates, and the tentative, possible, nervously casual rendezvous.

He watched as she walked away. She felt him looking and tossed him a knowing, accepting smile. A wave and a smile and she was gone.

The Old Pub

They sat around with long dark faces and matching drinks. The heavy ticking of the clock on the yellowed wall measured out the message of time wasted and worthless days. The depressing drink swilled the thoughts to wasted hours, wasted days, and wasted lives. It was not a convivial atmosphere.

The oldest of the group sat forward suddenly and took a decisive pull on his pint. Like a man who needed to get back to work, or to placate a waiting wife, he portrayed a momentary sense of urgency and agitation. But like the dusty bookshelves, it was in reality empty, and meaningless. The bar owner had intended to fill the shelves with leather-bound volumes from one of the big-house auctions. It had never been done. The sense of wasted time and unfulfilled possibility gripped the bar itself, and proclaimed the evidence in the empty shelves and the unkempt upholstery. Dirt accumulated in corners where the perfunctory swirl of the mop failed to reach. Blackness inhabited the grain of the wooden floor, and was old enough to be accepted as the mark of an unspoiled pub of the old school. In truth it was unspoiled, for that word implies the prior existence of something cleaner, better, neater, that was capable of being spoiled. The pub had never been that. Converted from an old spirit grocery store the original owner had made do with cheap solutions to every problem. The grocery counter was granted an extra layer of dark varnish. The racks that once held metal tins of biscuits gave way to pews from the old protestant church. Redundant bentwood chairs from the same source replaced the bins where potatoes and turnips once shed their soil. The dull green paint was judged to be adequate, and mismatched tables wobbled despite beermats wedged for temporary steadiness.

The drinker had a far-away look in his eye, and a wrinkling of the surrounding skin that could be mistaken for concentration on an inner world. 'A deep one that' – some were deceived into remarking. His companions ignored the flurry of misleading signals and continued in their dismal communal solitude. The old man sighed heavily and sat back on the pew, eyes returning to the grain of the table with its remaining evidence of the casual damp wipe of the barman's filthy cloth.

A visiting couple walked in and surveyed the scene with the expectant eyes and positive intention of the tourist. The dirt and gloom were judged to be atmospheric. The four silent drinkers were awarded the status of local colour. The barman looked up from his spread paper but did not stir. He was familiar with passing tourists who looked but did not stay. If they approached the counter well and good; if they sat down, they were welcome, and would no doubt eventually come to the counter.

A heavy camera was placed carefully on a corner table. The woman swept a hand over the seat of the bentwood chair before sitting. Determined smiles still clothed their faces, and conveyed the positive mindset of the well-intentioned visitors. The man looked at the foursome and nodded his head in a formal acknowledgement of their presence. In an overloud voice he inquired of his partner what she would like to drink. With her public perky bright voice she asked for a glass of white wine, but not Chardonnay.

The barman looked up glumly from his paper, and moved it to one side. The pencil stub that had been marking his chosen horses was laid carefully beside the paper during the temporary interruption. The man walked stiffly to the bar counter, his eyes scanning the unpromising shelf for any sign of wine bottles.

"A pint of Guinness please and a glass of white wine."

"Sorry now. There's no wine at all."

The man looked enquiringly at his companion, the eyes and eyebrows posing the question.

"Is there a dry sherry?"

The barman reached to the back row of the bottles on the shelf and produced a bottle of Bristol

Cream. A stained cloth wiped dust from the bottle's shoulder. He extracted the cork, reached for a whiskey glass, and paused. The spirit measure was too small. There hadn't been a call for the bigger measure for a while. He poured two spirit measures into the glass. Normally the pint of Guinness would have been started first, but he had been prepared for the couple to move on when the wine was mentioned. It happened when foreigners visited. So he hadn't risked starting the pint until the woman's drink had been agreed. The pint was poured with silent concentration, stopping with an inch of space left while the veils of bubbles swirled and rose and the liquid metamorphosed to its inky blackness and creamy white collar. The man looked on with approval, and turned to his companion with a knowing wink.

An ancient mechanical till dully rang its bell as the barman entered the two amounts and a whirr of machinery performed the addition. Money was handed over as the pint settled, and a few sticky coins were returned with a routine 'there you go now'. The pint was topped up and handed over before the blackness had completely settled. The tourist took the two glasses to the side table and returned to pick up two beer-mats from the counter. The transactions complete, he cocked his head to watch the drink finish its settling and blackening. His companion dutifully watched and waited before reaching for her sherry. At last the blackness was sufficiently uniform and they raised their glasses, clinked, and chimed 'Slainte'.

The four silent drinkers had observed the entire transaction with a distant disguised interest.

There might have been a heavy glass partition separating the table of four from the two. It did not seem that any communication was expected or appropriate.

Conversation was muted. The couple quietly discussed the guidebook and the best route to the town where they planned to stay the night. The woman read aloud the brief description of the village the pub served, and suggested a visit to the ruined abbey on the outskirts. The subject of lunch was raised, but they agreed silently that they would not even ask in the pub if sandwiches were available. When asked how her sherry was, the woman did not answer directly but conveyed with a warning frown that the subject should not be pursued. A sense of awkward determination to finish the drinks replaced the earlier positivism.

"Ah well, that'll be the rain then," commented one of the four drinkers.

"Aye, 'twas expected all right."

"Sure it was expected since Sunday."

"Well there it is then."

"And that's a fact."

"I see young Jamie hasn't cut a bit of the field yet."

"You couldn't tell him."

"That's a fact."

They all had a pull at their pints and relapsed into ruminative silence.

The barman's pencil made an occasional scratching sound as another horse was underlined. A grunt accompanied each mark, as if he was achieving satisfaction from the complex decisions he was making. It did not convey any sign of pleasure. The concentration was dutiful and thorough, but without expectation or excitement.

At last the couple finished their drinks. The woman looked around for the toilets and was about to ask, but changed her mind and her mouth closed again. The proper little mouth-smile returned, and with it the air of slightly put-upon long-suffering that her companion knew well and dreaded. The man returned the empty glasses to the bar counter and thanked the preoccupied barman. He helped the woman sling the backpack onto her shoulders, and carefully picked up his expensive camera. Had the barman been looking, he would have received a silent question as the man looked at the camera and looked around the bar. But the moment passed.

"Good day to you then," the man offered as they pulled open the half-glass door.

"Aye. Good luck," the barman responded without looking up.

The door swung closed behind them, and the men watched the shapes disappear down the street, wobbling indistinctly through the screen of wrinkled glass that kept the interior private.

"Well what did you make of that?"

"Did you see the face on her?"

"And where do you think they blew in from?"

"Did you see the cut of yer woman when she didn't get her wine?"

"I doubt they'll be back for another one here Gerry."

"Thank god for that. Did you see the look of

her when he asked her about the sherry?"

"O that boy hasn't his sorrows to seek I'm telling you. He'll be getting an earful by now all right."

ALSO BY JACK DYLAN

The Turkish Trap
Alex loves sailing, he also loves Maggie, but tricked into smuggling he's locked in a Turkish jail.

Against a Mediterranean backdrop, with action in London, Dublin and Edinburgh, The Turkish Trap is the tense and intriguing story of Alex's desperate fight to undo his past mistakes and rescue his future.

The Russian Deal
Katja wants James. She isn't the only one. But the other one wants him dead.

When James and his team develop a technology that threatens a Russian Oligarch's big deal, two unsavoury hit-men are dispatched to England with murderous intent.

Printed in Dunstable, United Kingdom